Clai

Hannah’s Pray… from Desolation

How one desperate prayer rattled heaven and changed the world.

Part 1 of the Life of David Series from 1 & 2 Samuel.

Get a free download of Hannah’s Prayer when you sign up for D. Richard Ferguson’s Reader’s Group at www.DRichardFerguson.com.

Other books by D. Richard Ferguson

Escape from Paradise: A Christian Adventure Novel

Book 1 in the *Walk with the Wind* Series

Deeper Knowledge of God: Meditations on 76 Attributes

180 daily meditations on 76 attributes of God to help you increase your delight in the Lord

Lost in Prayer: Guided Prayer and Meditation on God’s Word

Guided prayer and meditation on Scripture. A 40-day devotional

Wise Counsel: Applying the Word of God to Life’s Problems

Find solutions in God’s Word for depression, anxiety, bipolar, anger, and many other common

At War
with the Wind

The Fight for Abigail

Book 2 of the Walk with the Wind Series

D. Richard Ferguson

www.DRichardFerguson.com

Published by Food For Your Soul Ministries
Applying the Word of God to the Hearts of Men and Women

Acknowledgements

I wrote the *Walk with the Wind* series to dramatize biblical principles I have learned to make sure I don't forget them. The principles came from many sources, too many to list, but some of the most direct allusions are to teaching from John Piper and Thomas Watson.

Much of the material about escaping bondage came directly from sermons by John Piper on the subject, including some direct quotations. I am deeply indebted to Mr. Piper for the incalculable impact his teaching has made on my spiritual life.

It was from Thomas Watson's book, *Repentance*, that I drew many principles portrayed in this series. I highly recommend his book on the subject.

Credits

Thank you to Faith Reeves for drawing all the maps in both volumes.

And thanks to the team who helped launch *At War with the Wind.* Without their work, it's likely you, dear reader, never would have heard of the book.

Jim Adam
Kelly Barr
Josiah Ferguson
Tracy Ferguson
Gene Geurink
Stephanie Geurink
Pamela Hart
Janeen Honsey
Tammy Horvath
Jennie Johnson
RaTasha Lawson
Abigail Martin
Faith Reeves
Janet Ruth
Patty Schrock
Sandra Stewart
Carolyn-Nicole Stroud
Dana Yost
Bonnie Yost

"He who is full loathes honey,
but to the hungry
even what is bitter tastes sweet."

\- *Proverbs 27:7*

BOOK 2

THE FIGHT FOR ABIGAIL

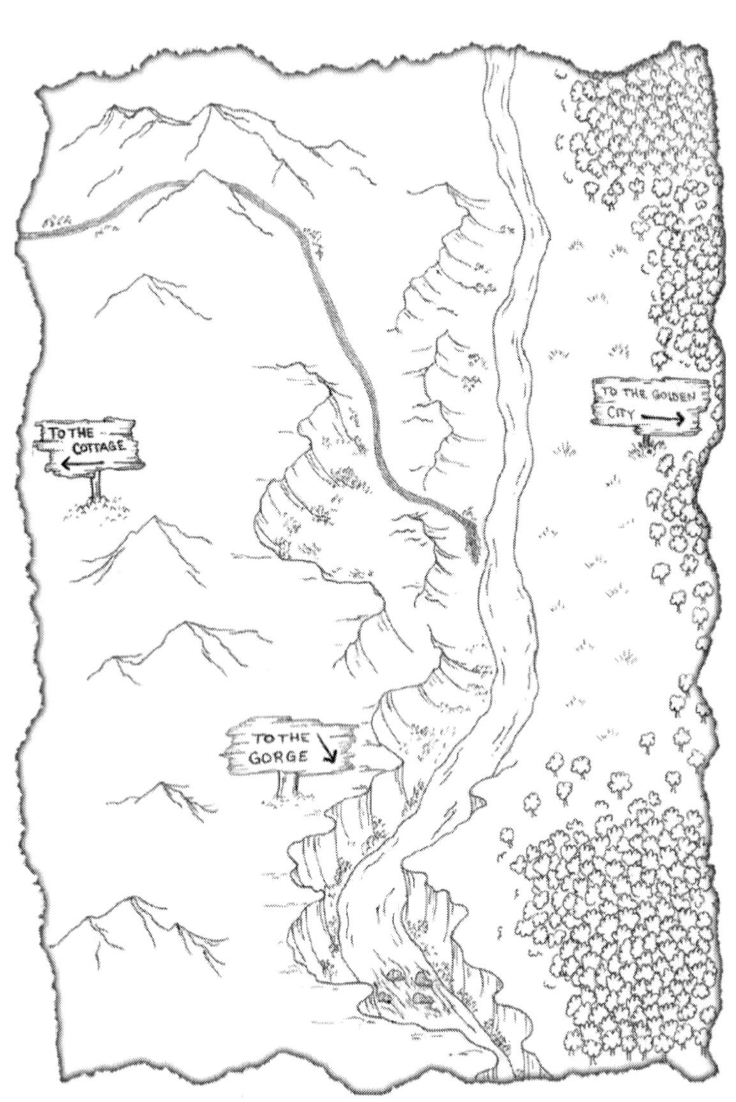

TO THE COTTAGE
TO THE GOLDEN CITY
TO THE GORGE

Chapter 1

Sweat beaded on Watson's face as he imagined his sister in the clutches of the enemy. Was it already too late for her? *Why did I wait so long?*

Watson's mind always churned with planning and strategizing, but this was another level. Rescuing his sister rose above any mission he had ever undertaken. Plans coalesced in thoughts as he gathered supplies in the boathouse with Layth and Kailyn. Rigging, crossing the river, and carrying the boat to the boathouse on the other side shouldn't take more than a half-hour. If they didn't stop for rest, the journey up through the grasslands could be done in—

A distant roar interrupted his calculations. The moment they stepped outside, they saw it—a flash flood tumbling down from the north. In the few minutes they had been in the boathouse, the river had swollen to double its volume and was well over its banks.

Crestfallen, Watson studied the torrent. "It's impossible. We would never make it across. We would be swept into the gorge." He shook his head. "We will have to wait it out."

The delay felt like a prison sentence to Watson. Every second that passed was a second lost. But he saw no other option.

"Where's Kailyn?" Layth asked.

The men returned to the boathouse and found her inside, tugging at a boat.

"What are you doing?" Watson objected. "We cannot—"

"We're going," she said, without looking up.

Watson stepped close. "Kailyn, stop." He placed his hand on hers.

She stopped pulling and dropped her head.

"Believe me," he said. "I want to get to Abigail as much as you. But we will do her no good if we are all dead. Flash floods never last long. We simply need to wait it out."

Kailyn's face hardened like steel. "Do what you want. I'm going. If you won't help, I'll swim across."

Watson knew her well enough to know she would do it. And he knew the river well enough to know she would not survive.

"The gorge is four miles of continuous, deadly whitewater. There is no stopping. And the rapids are unnavigable even at normal water levels. Right now the volume is easily seven or eight thousand cubic feet per second. At that volume—"

She held up her hand. “Did the Ruler send us on this mission or not? Every hour we delay could be the hour time runs out for Abigail. I’d rather die trying to save her than sit around here waiting.”

Layth shifted his jaw, shot an apologetic look at Watson, and carved a path toward the boat. He grabbed a handle and began dragging it out of the boathouse. Kailyn held Watson in her gaze for another long moment, then followed. Watson hesitated, then fell in line.

Layth took his place on the left front and Kailyn across from him, while Watson stationed himself in the stern to guide. They pointed the bow upstream at a steep ferry angle to ensure they would make it across without being carried too far downstream.

Watson shouted a command as they pushed out from shore and they all paddled in sync, struggling to maintain the angle. By their fourth stroke, the main current caught the bow and spun the raft so they faced straight downstream.

With some effort, Watson managed to turn back toward the east shore, but the three paddlers were no match for the accelerating current. With each stroke eastward, the river carried them another fifty feet downstream. Kailyn looked back at Watson. He saw in her eyes a moment of terror, followed immediately by the same steeled determination as at the boathouse.

The river narrowed, and the boat picked up speed.

*****

"He's back," Lucius said, nodding toward the grasslands.

Adramelech, the legion commander, stepped out to meet the dark spirit as he and his detachment approached the black timber. "Report, Anzu?"

"Success, sir. They tried to cross but dropped into the gorge. You won't have to worry about those three anymore."

Adramelech's lips parted in a rare grin. "Impressive."

Timing the flood and raising the flow just enough to prevent them from crossing but not so high as to stop them from trying were difficult feats. He had been skeptical about Anzu's ability to pull all that off—especially given the unpredictability of the Mighty Wind.

Lucius, who normally deprecated everything Anzu did, held his tongue. Adramelech sensed that both his lieutenants felt relieved to be done with Layth. They feared him, though neither would ever admit it. Indeed, even Adramelech had been uneasy about possibly having to face the powerful man of faith. With him and the other two out of the way, Adramelech's plans for Abigail should be safe.

*****

Watson, Layth, and Kailyn knew they would not likely survive what was coming. All three were ready to face death and the final judgment that followed. Their greatest anxiety was not their impending demise.

It was the much worse fate Abigail would face if she were not rescued in time and was taken with the city.

Throughout the tight box canyon there were not only powerful currents and crushing rapids but also sharp, jagged rocks scattered throughout the river. Being pitched out of the boat at any point in this canyon could prove fatal in multiple ways.

They had only seconds to prepare for the approaching ordeal. Hitting a large rapid at an angle would result in capsizing. And there were many rapids in the gorge that would flip the boat even if they hit them straight on. They must be avoided at all cost. Watson ruddered the boat to face directly downstream as they dropped into the mouth of the gorge.

"Dig in!" Watson shouted, as a wall of water slammed the boat. Kailyn sputtered and tried to catch a breath after the blast in her face. Wet strands of Layth's hair whipped side to side as he tested the limits of his paddle in a furious forward stroke.

Kailyn caught Watson's attention with a wave of her paddle. He couldn't hear her shouts over the roaring river, but she pointed to a sharp, triangular rock jutting several feet out of the roiling torrent dead ahead.

"I see it." Watson used the force of a diagonal wave and a powerful left draw to get the angle he wanted and shouted, "Hard forward!" He held the angle while Layth and Kailyn stroked furiously to avoid the deadly obstacle. "Hard forward!" he roared again.

The bow cleared, but the stern bumped and spun the boat, nearly knocking Watson into the river.

Now they faced directly upstream, plunging backward toward the next rapid. There was no time to correct. “Backpaddle!” Watson commanded, hoping to punch through the wall of whitewater with a strong backstroke.

The boat accelerated, dropped, and slammed into the boiling wave like a brick wall. Kailyn slid backward, fell headfirst into the current, and was swept away. Her head popped up momentarily, then disappeared.

Watson’s knowledge of the river now became his enemy because he understood how hopeless their situation had suddenly become. Down a paddler, they were heading into even larger rapids than the ones that had given them such a thrashing. He froze, paralyzed with dread.

Layth seemed to sense Watson’s fear. He pointed straight at Watson and shouted over the roar of the river, “Don’t forget!”

The Ruler’s promise at the banquet hall cascaded through Watson’s memory. *I will be with you.* While his body remained in the doomed boat, his heart rested in the promise room, comfortably seated in the overstuffed fear-not-for-I-am-with-you chair. Peace flooded his soul. As violent as this death might be, the Ruler would be with him. And when it was over, he would be with the Ruler in the new world forever. “I am ready.”

The river poured into a massive cataract next to the left shore. Without a third paddler, Watson and Layth had no chance of missing it. The boil swallowed the craft like a lion devouring its prey.

The boat remained upright but stalled in the hydraulic. A surge of whitewater exploded under the boat, pushing it backward to the cascade rushing down into the hole. When the boat collided with the current, it lurched up on its side, dumping Watson into the boil. Layth clung to the high side, which slammed down on a flat rock on the shore.

Watson was pulled so far under, the pressure hurt his ears. He flailed and kicked but didn't even know which direction was up as the torrent tumbled him and slammed him against rocks.

Desperate for air, he finally bobbed up and barely had time for a gasp before another wave shoved him under. He surfaced again and caught a glance of Layth lying on the rock, eyes vacant, body limp.

The last thing Watson saw before a current pulled him under again was the boat being pushed into a jagged, undercut cliff where it was ripped to pieces.

Then, blackness.

Chapter 2

Every room, every wall, every piece of furniture in the Ruler's massive headquarters took on a whole new look to Adam. After going through the blood room and promise room, he was a new man. What had appeared before as ordinary features of the building now shone with brilliance that surpassed anything in the golden city.

The Ruler stepped into the hallway and gave a sideways nod toward the end of the hall. "Come. We have something for you."

Adam followed, and they came to a room marked "Assignments." As the Ruler put his hand on the latch, Adam stepped back. "It sounds like a hurricane in there."

The Ruler smiled. "It is. And he has a gift for you."

"He?" Adam had sensed the wind was more than a natural force, but … *he?* "Are you saying the wind is a … person?"

The Ruler laughed. "The Mighty Wind is the ultimate person. He *defines* personhood. His power and wisdom are the source of all personalities, including yours. He is the one who brought you here and preserved your life on the way. He drew you here because he loves you."

As they entered the room, Adam expected to be pinned to the wall by the roaring gale. Instead, the power of the wind held him up and stabilized him.

Just as the chain had earlier, a box materialized in the Ruler's hand, wrapped in paper and a bow.

He held it out to Adam. "Open it!" His eager tone made Adam wonder if the gift was as much for the Ruler as it was for Adam.

Like a child on his birthday, Adam tore off the paper revealing a hand-carved wooden chest—small enough to hold in his hand. He opened it, looked inside, frowned, and lifted questioning eyes to the Ruler.

"Look again," said the Ruler.

Adam felt the inside. When he withdrew his fingers, he held a pair of glasses. The thin frames had blended with the inside of the chest, and the lenses were so crystal clear they were barely visible.

"Put them on."

Adam obeyed, wondering if perhaps they would give him the clear vision of the world that the little one's salve had given him—but without the nearsightedness.

He examined the chest in his hand. It appeared the same with or without the glasses.

"Do you still have the piece Abigail gave you?"

Adam retrieved it from his pocket. But he didn't need to read the inscription. He had it memorized. "The banquet is like a treasure hidden in a field ...."

"Look at it through the glasses."

Adam studied the piece as he had so many times before. "I see some colors—the same ones I saw before."

"You see the colors on the surface. Look harder."

Adam scrutinized the piece from every angle. He held it up to the light, turned it over in his hand, rubbed it with his thumb … "What am I looking for?"

"There is much more to see. Keep looking."

Adam gave up six times, and six times the Ruler repeated the instruction. "Keep looking."

It was more than an hour later when Adam finally saw something he hadn't noticed before. A thin line, barely detectable, along the left side.

"Is that a crack?"

"It's a seam," said the Ruler.

Adam inspected the line and realized the piece had been folded. He pulled it open. Now four times its original size, the piece displayed a rainbow of prismatic luminescence within the folds. Warmth filled Adam's chest. The wind swirled around him and his skin dripped with blue fluid.

The Ruler explained. "Every piece of the cottage has been folded a thousand times. Any one of my people can find a seam and discover new colors if they look hard enough. The wind will reveal it to them. But the glasses you have been given will enable you to discover many more seams than others can find. I want my people to see them. The wind gave you these glasses because your task is to show my people colors they can't find. That's the meaning of your new name." The Ruler pointed to the bar hanging from Adam's neck.

Adam took the bar between his fingers and looked again at the inscription—*David.*

"He was a shepherd of my people. A shepherd's job is to lead, protect, and especially, to feed my sheep. Every time you unfold a piece of the cottage and cause someone to see the colors, you are placing food from my table into their mouths."

The Ruler took the bar in his fingers and flipped it over to face inward against Adam's skin. "They will know your name in time when they discover it in your character—not by reading it on an inscription."

Adam carefully placed the glasses back in the chest.

"No," said the Ruler. "You must wear them at all times. They are your weapon, and you must become skilled in their use." The Ruler's expression darkened. "You will soon fight a battle in which your life and the lives of others will be lost if you do not master that weapon."

*****

The ranks of warriors stood at attention before their legendary commander, Adramelech. He sensed their tension.

Adramelech raised his hand and silenced the legion of evil spirits then turned to his right and bowed. Gasps permeated the ranks as they all followed his lead, showing homage as the prince of darkness himself approached the platform.

As the prince drew near, Adramelech struggled to breathe—every nerve alert, every muscle taught to the point of pain. *This must be what it feels like for humans when they tremble in our presence.*

Warriors throughout the ranks wheezed and choked. Some vomited even as they struggled to maintain their poise. The massive, hideous lord of darkness ascended the platform, his body twisted, his face distorted, emitting a toxic stench. He ran his deadly gaze across the assembled spirits as blood and bits of human flesh dripped from his fangs.

Words began to slither from his throat. "Good progress has been made in our efforts to take Abigail and to keep our hold on Adam." His gaze turned ice cold. "However, I am not satisfied. Your failures with Watson, Layth, and Kailyn are inexcusable."

Anzu shot a chastising glance at Dagon.

The prince's face burned red. He fixed his gaze on Anzu and expelled a putrid stench with his slow, deliberate words. "Am I boring you, little imp?"

Anzu stiffened and locked his gaze forward, avoiding eye contact with the prince.

The evil behemoth returned his gaze to the ranks. “Do you take this mission lightly because you think it is merely two souls? Think again. Abigail is highly esteemed by many—many who are now vulnerable. Charles Baxter is on the cusp of discouragement and has not sought help. Abigail is a domino in a plan that could bring down the most powerful banquet hall in the region.”

“If this effort fails,” he added with a lowered pitch that made sweat bead on Adramelech’s scaly hide, “any warrior who has put forth anything short of full effort, I assure you, will regret his dereliction.”

*****

Immersed in the water alongside Watson, Sol lifted his charge just enough to keep his face above water. The guardian had followed the Ruler’s orders to the letter. *You may preserve Watson’s life and minister hope and strength, but do not interfere with the test.*

*****

Bruised, battered, and barely alive, Watson drifted out of the gorge where the river opened into a calm stretch. He probed his body for broken bones and wondered how he had survived.

From the center of the river, he turned to his right. A spark of new life ignited in him when he saw the haven of the west shore—a place of safety where he could recover in the high country.

But as he started swimming in that direction, he remembered Kailyn. The image of her steeled determination at the boathouse appeared in his mind with such vividness, he wondered if perhaps a guardian was present, whispering in his ear.

He stopped swimming. Should he continue the mission alone?

Reaching the orchard from this end of the gorge would take significantly longer than the original journey—if it was even possible. The already slim chances of making it to Abigail in time were now even worse. Especially without Layth and Kailyn.

Additionally, he now understood something of the degree of opposition he faced. This had been no random storm. The king of this world was serious about keeping his hold on Abigail, and if it meant killing Watson or anyone else, he wouldn't hesitate.

On the other hand, Watson loved his sister. And he had been sent by the Ruler. When the Ruler commissioned a task, giving up because of steep odds was not a tenable excuse.

He turned toward the east bank. Fatigue and discouragement sapped the whispers of strength remaining in him. He wanted to simply go limp and float wherever the current took him. But again he recalled Kailyn's courage. With a lurch of resolve, his mind gave the order for his legs to kick. But were they responding? Numb from the frigid water and the beating he took in the gorge, he couldn't feel his limbs.

A hundred times, it seemed, he ordered his body forward before his hand finally grasped a stone along the eastern shore.

He rolled himself out of the river. Splayed on his back, the dark clouds forming above were the last image to paint his thoughts before closing eyelids darkened his world.

He woke with a chill. *How long was I out?* The same storm clouds swirled above. *Not too long. Good. I need to get moving.*

Countless bruises and lacerations screamed their objections as he labored to stand. He scrambled along the rocky shore, working his way upstream to find any sign of his friends—or their remains.

A familiar voice reached his ears. "Watson!"

He lifted his eyes to a sight so welcome it brought an involuntary laugh. "Kailyn!"

His dear friend leaned against a boulder, torn and bedraggled, her ebony hair plastered in long swaths to her face.

"You made it!" he said, climbing through the boulders that stood between them. The two friends embraced as Kailyn's tears ran freely onto Watson's shoulder.

As they exchanged stories, Watson shared the grim news about Layth. "It didn't look like he survived the impact. The way his arm hung off the side of that rock—he was most certainly unconscious. And the shoreline there is a sheer cliff. The only way off that rock would be to jump back into the river."

For the next several hours they searched the banks for his body. By late afternoon they came to the grievous conclusion that it had been swept downstream or caught up in a logjam. There was no point in staying here any longer. They had a mission to accomplish.

Before them lay the long trek northward through the canyon lands, and then east to the orchard. With the steep canyon walls, cliffs, and loose rock, this journey wouldn't be any easier, or safer, than the trip down the river had been. In addition, the heaviness of heart from the loss of their dear friend Layth made even the easiest path feel arduous.

An hour into the canyon lands, their conversation halted momentarily as they reached the far side of the gully they had been crossing. They scanned the canyon wall before them, looking for a way up. There were only two options—scale the cliffs to the left or crawl up the slide-rock area to the right.

Watson rubbed his chin. "It would be unwise for both of us to climb that slide area—too risky."

"Agreed. I have more experience with technical climbing. I'll see if I can make it up the cliff while you try the slide-rock. If one of us doesn't make it, the other can continue the mission."

Kailyn drew a deep breath as she studied the wall to map a route. She had made some difficult climbs in the past, but never without ropes and never on crumbling sandstone like this. She had to choose each handhold and foothold carefully, balancing the importance of finding solid holds with the urgency of moving quickly. If she climbed too slowly, her strength would run out before she reached the top.

She stood back, picked a line, and began the climb. Thoughts of Abigail propelled her up the cliff. Why had she allowed her friend to be taken? *I just sat and enjoyed the banquet while a life was being destroyed.* She pounded the rock face with her fist, then climbed faster.

Soon she felt her muscles reaching their limit. With each new toehold, the tremble in her legs increased. She looked down. *Eighty feet. Maybe a hundred.* No chance of surviving a fall. Her muscles screamed for rest. She looked up. Only halfway.

She could no longer be selective with her handholds. She must reach the top as quickly as possible and hope the holds would bear her weight.

*****

Watson started up the only route that had a line of sight all the way to the top. But the slide-rock soon gave way beneath him. He managed to keep his feet, but with a fresh array of bruises and cuts on his legs.

His methodical, problem-solving mind analyzed every possible route. *That way? No. Over there? Too steep. Could I angle across ...* He shook his head. All the routes within view were impossible. And the lines that looked like he might be able to handle all were obscured by shrubs. They could lead to a dead end, stranding him half way up with no way back down. Down climbing is far more difficult than ascending.

His heart pounded. If Kailyn made it up, she wouldn't be able to come back down to him. But this isn't a journey she should take on her own. *I've got to find a way up.*

*****

Grasping a root, Kailyn pulled herself onto a ledge at the top of the cliff. She rolled to her back to catch her breath and allow her burning muscles to finally rest.

When she had regained enough strength to walk, she stood and angled eastward along the top of the ridge to the place she expected Watson to arrive.

There was no sign of him.

"Watson!" The only response was the echo of her voice in the canyon. A lump rose in her throat.

She ran along the ridgeline shouting for her friend, searching the ground for footprints, listening for a response.

She returned to where she had come up, then closed her eyes. *How far did I walk from where I left him to where I started climbing?* She formed a mental picture, then paced off the distance the best she could.

She looked over the side but there were too many shrubs to see very far. The ground lay completely undisturbed.

She cupped her hands around her mouth and drew the deepest breath she could take in. "*Wat-suuuun!*"

Chapter 3

This time, Kailyn heard a voice from below. "Down here."

She followed down a narrow, winding path that terminated at a level area peppered with bushes. Watson sat, sweating and staring at the dirt. Footprints covered the ground as if he had been pacing.

Kailyn put her hands on her hips. "Taking a rest?"

Watson looked up with a forced smile, opened his mouth, but then closed it again.

Kailyn sat beside him.

"So, I guess you made it up okay?" Watson said.

"Tough climb, but I managed. Did you have any trouble?"

Watson lowered his head again.

"What's wrong, Watson?" Then she noticed a blackberry bush a few feet away. "Oh, did you …"

He lifted his head and drew a deep breath. "Yes, I sampled a couple berries. Not like a full meal or anything. I just … thought … I … I probably shouldn't have, but I saw the bush, and ..."

Kailyn sat in silence for a few moments, then placed a hand on his back. "It was a mistake. Live and learn, right?"

He pressed his lips together. "Yes. Live and learn."

From atop the ridge, another voice sounded. "Amen to that."

Watson and Kailyn both stood to see who had spoken. Silhouetted against the twilight sky stood a man in tattered clothes. Kailyn's training told her to move several paces to her right. If the stranger attacked, the separation would make them two targets instead of one.

But she ignored the impulse and stayed in place. The man's friendly tone and non-threatening posture set her at ease.

"Are you okay?" called the stranger.

"We're fine," Kailyn said.

The man worked his way down the path. "Couldn't help but overhear your conversation. It sounds like you're both cottage people. I am too! I came to the lowlands to visit a friend but got a little lost. It's good to see some friendly faces."

The stranger paused at a strawberry plant, bent down to retrieve a berry, and popped it in his mouth. "You don't mind, do you?"

"Difficult to resist when one is in the lowlands," Watson said.

"I'm glad to finally meet someone who isn't so uptight about small things. The Ruler never meant for us to live in legalistic bondage."

Watson nodded and plucked a blackberry like it was a daily occurrence. Kailyn felt the impulse to do the same. Not that she wanted any fruit, but it seemed rude not to join the stranger in partaking.

*****

Watson and Kailyn had both received extensive instruction about the battle in the spiritual realm. And both excelled in their ability to sense unseen activity. But the winsome stranger had set them at such ease that neither had an inkling of the skirmish taking place in that moment.

A dark power emerged from inside the stranger. In an instant, K-lion, Kailyn's guardian, lunged in front of Kailyn to shield her. Watson's guardian, Sol, rushed the power, leaving Watson exposed. It was a calculated risk. He knew two guardians would be no match for a regional power. But Sol had unusual speed. If he could catch the power by surprise, maybe …

The power easily parried Sol's strike, sending him sliding into a clump of bushes. Before he could recover, scores of warriors sprang from hiding places on every side and surrounded him. In an instant, the regimen of warriors had K-lion and Sol in custody.

The power drew his bow and fired two arrows in quick succession. The first sank deep into Watson's chest, just missing his heart. The second flew toward Kailyn, but she sensed the evil presence and dove to the side. The arrow glanced off her knee, leaving a deep gash.

Sol thrashed against his captors as the evil power approached Watson and Kailyn.

*****

"I just wanted to make sure you were okay down here," said the stranger. "I don't know where you're headed, but I wouldn't recommend trying to go down that." He gestured to the steep downslope. "That'd be some rough going."

"Tell me about it," Watson replied. "I just climbed up from down there."

"What?" The man leaned over the side. "How in the world did you make it up that slide-rock? You're a brave man." Shaking his head, he turned back to Watson. "How did you get down there in the first place?"

"We were attempting to cross the river and were swept into the gorge. We had to climb out from the bottom."

The man's wide eyes widened further. "You went through the gorge? Whoa! I've never heard of anyone surviving that stretch of river." He plucked another berry. "Either you're amazing paddlers or the luckiest two people on the planet."

Watson took a handful of berries from the same bush.

"Watson—" Kailyn started.

"I'm Watson," he said, extending free hand. The stranger shook it. "And this is Kailyn."

"Pleased to meet you. I'm Michael.

*****

Drawing another arrow from his quiver, the dark power set it on the string, drew it back, and pointed it directly at Watson's heart.

A blinding flash exploded from the ridge above. Streams of orange and red light shot out like a spider web, and behind that, a bright, royal blue glow. The warriors dropped their weapons and covered their eyes. A massive javelin struck the dark power from behind with such force it sent him headlong down the hill where he disappeared into a thorny berry patch.

As the light subsided, the warriors removed their hands from their eyes. They wilted when they saw the man who stood above them.

*****

Watson dropped the berries, startled by a booming voice from the slope above. "Live by Judas desires and you'll die!"

Kailyn drew an excited breath. "Layth! You're alive!"

Layth moved down the path, eyeing the stranger with the caution of a deer in lion country.

Kailyn ran to Layth and threw her arms around him. "We searched the end of the gorge for you. We thought … How did you …?"

"When I came to, I was on a rock between the water and the cliff. Wasn't goin' back in that river. So … I climbed. Figured it was my only hope."

Kailyn raised a brow. "You climbed the canyon wall?"

Layth shrugged. "It was windy."

His smile flattened when he turned and eyed the berries at Watson's feet. "Speaking of wind, are you walking with him Watson?"

The stranger rolled his eyes. "It was a couple of berries. We all make mistakes. The Father understands that."

Layth laid a hard stare on the stranger. "Was someone talking to you?"

For the briefest moment, the stranger clenched his teeth, then relaxed—but stood his ground.

Kailyn took note. This stranger was clearly a man who could handle himself. Anyone else would wilt under a threatening word from battle-hardened redhead.

Layth turned to Watson. "Have you forgotten the warning—that if any man says, 'I will be safe, even though I persist in going my own way'—the Father will never be willing to forgive him?"

Shoulders slumped and head down, Watson kept silent.

Kailyn could relate. She also felt the quills as her heart ran against the grain of those words—especially the last phrase, *the Father will never be willing to forgive*.

*****

The dark power regained his footing and started up the hill toward the three friends. Warriors blanketed the hillside.

Again, the power spewed his attacks into Watson's ears. *Why do you think you could help Abigail escape? You can't even resist a couple berries. Get the log out of your own eye before you try to help someone else.*

The warriors nearby salivated as they saw Watson's heart falter under the assault.

Watson dropped his shield and the power intensified the thrashing. *Face it. You failed. You were entrusted with an important task, and you couldn't even cross the river without botching the whole operation. And now, with your own sister's life on the line, you're sitting around eating berries. Do you seriously think you can be the one to carry out the Ruler's work?*

The power stood over Watson and pressed his foot down on his neck while a dozen warriors surrounded Layth, weapons drawn.

*****

Layth spoke with urgency. "Watson, resist, and he will flee!"

Watson looked up at Layth with confused, pleading eyes. "How? I'm pinned."

"Wash your hands. Purify your heart. Grieve, mourn, and wail. Change your laughter to mourning and your joy to gloom. Humble yourself. Return to the Ruler, and he will return to you."

"Grieve, mourn, and wail?" said the stranger. "Isn't that a little melodramatic? It's not like he committed murder or something."

Layth turned back to the stranger and stepped close.

The man tensed and slipped his right hand inside his long coat.

"Layth!" Kailyn said, fearing the stranger would produce a weapon.

Layth steeled his jaw. He moved even closer and kept his tone even. "Take a walk."

The stranger flushed, narrowed his gaze, and eyed Layth up and down. "Who are you to—"

"I'm nobody. Your problem isn't who I am. It's who sent me. I know who you are. And I know you are powerful—in this world. But you know that the one who sent me can turn you into a grease spot. So—*Get. Lost*."

Kailyn thought she heard a deep growl rise from inside the man. He faced Layth for a beat, then turned and headed up the hill.

Layth faced Watson and Kailyn. "Do you know the difference between satisfying your appetite and spoiling it?"

They were silent for a moment, waiting for Layth to go on. But he only folded his arms, waiting for an answer.

"They are the same," Watson said. "In either case, food is eaten and hunger diminished."

"Right. So then why do we call one spoiling and the other satisfying?"

The light began to dawn for Kailyn. She spoke as one speaks when puzzle pieces in her mind are assembling themselves with each word she utters. "Appetite is satisfied … when we eat something … good. Appetite is spoiled when … we eat something bad and no longer desire the good thing."

Layth pointed at Kailyn as if she had just won a prize. "And the fruit doesn't just spoil your appetite. It damages your taste buds. And that's serious, because the Ruler's food doesn't nourish you unless you can taste it."

He went on. "This isn't just about nibbling a few berries. It's a betrayal. Just as a man's marital desires belong only to his wife, our appetite for life and joy belongs only to the Ruler. His claim on our hearts is greater than a wife's claim on her husband's."

Layth held up his wrists. "Do you remember the Ruler's scars?"

"Of course," Watson said. "He nearly lost his hands."

"That's right. And he didn't take those wounds just to *pay* for your evils. He also suffered to *prevent* them. That's how much he desires your purity and eagerness to do good."

Watson stood. "He's right. This is not an inconsequential matter. The moment we get back from this mission, my first priority will be to confess to the Ruler and—"

"No! Not when the mission is over. Now." Layth stepped closer to Watson. "Don't let the sun go down a single time on your guilt. From the moment you eat fruit until you go before the Father, you allow the evil one to hold a place inside you. Don't you understand how—"

"Watson and I both stumbled," Kailyn said. "We were wrong, and we need to make things right with the Ruler as soon as we can. But we can't return now. The Ruler sent us here on a mission, and we must be faithful to carry it out. Time is running out for Abigail."

*****

The dark power continued to batter Watson. *The Father is angry. Now is not the time to go seeking forgiveness. Give it some time. Let things cool off. He's not going to want to see you right now.*

Watson squeezed his eyes closed, trapping his tears. Fresh stabs of self-loathing ripped through his soul. Normally he could parry such arguments in his sleep. But the pain of failure and regret paralyzed his will, leaving him defenseless.

The power went on. *The Father will forgive you in time, but wait for his wrath to subside. For now, do some things you know are pleasing to him. Curry some favor. Then, when this misstep is a little farther in the past, you can stand before him. But don't go asking for his favor now—it's too soon.*

Watson summoned his remaining strength and pulled a tiny dagger from his boot. The blade sparked with purple light. One edge bore the inscription—*Today, if you hear his voice, do not harden your heart.* The opposite edge read, *Seek the Lord while he may be found.*

"I am going back," Watson announced. "Right now."

The power's eyes widened and an involuntary whimper escaped his lips. He lurched backward, turned, and ran straight downhill, trampling his minions who also retreated, falling and tumbling in a chaotic, desperate effort to escape.

*****

"I guess the power is afraid of pocketknives," joked Big Red, Layth's guardian.

"He'd better be," thundered a voice from atop the ridge. The guardians and the friends all knew that voice. The power's terror was not from Watson or the knife. It was from the one who gave Watson that knife—the only one greater than the dark powers. The Ruler of the kings of the earth stood against the twilight sky in all his magnificent glory.

Chapter 4

Kailyn and Layth both dropped to their knees in joyful worship. Watson rose to his knees as relief, sorrow, and happiness to see the Ruler all erupted into uncontrollable sobs.

A moment earlier, Watson had been convinced the Ruler wouldn't even want to see him. But not only was he willing, he came all this way to rescue Watson. The Ruler's words from the banquet hall rang again in his mind. *I will be with you.*

The Ruler took Watson's hand and pulled him to his feet, instantly healing the wound from the arrow. Watson threw his arms around his beloved king and buried his face in the Ruler's chest.

The Ruler whispered to Watson what was already obvious from his embrace, "I have spoken to the Father. He loves you so much. *All is forgiven!*"

No words could have been sweeter to Watson's ears.

The Ruler touched Kailyn and healed her wound as well. Then he turned to Layth. "It's okay. I know what you're thinking—you can say it."

Layth let out a hearty belly laugh. "All right, I'll ask. You brought food, right?"

Watson and Kailyn joined in the laughter, and the Ruler smiled and gave Layth a nod. "Build a fire."

The friends sat late into the night around the campfire, sharing stories, laughing, marveling at the Ruler's wisdom, and gorging themselves on the delicious meal.

After the most restful, rejuvenating night's sleep they had experienced in a long time, all three woke to the aromas of the food the Ruler had already prepared.

It was a simple breakfast by the Ruler's standards—eggs and bacon, French toast, and muffins.

Watson swallowed the last bite from his plate and sat back. "That most thoroughly hit the spot."

He glanced at the bush he had eaten from the day before and cocked his head.

"What's wrong?" Layth asked.

"The berries. They …"

He went to the bush for a closer look. After circling it, he knelt and moved several branches aside, inspecting the fruit.

Layth set his plate down and squinted at Watson. "What is it?"

"These are not berries. They appear to be … goat head burrs." He touched one and jerked his hand back. "Ouch!" A drop of blood formed where it had punctured his skin, and he shook his hand as he felt stinging poison from the burr.

He turned to a nearby grapevine. The clusters were not grapes, but scorpions. The strawberry plant the stranger had eaten from moved. He crushed a strawberry with his shoe and maggots spilled out, along with a putrid stench that drove him several steps back.

"Not very appetizing when you can see it clearly, is it?" asked the Ruler. "Can you see now why I don't want you to eat the 'fruit' over here?"

"*That* is what I ate yesterday?"

The Ruler gave a solemn nod. Then he smiled. "I will never, ever forbid anything good. You will see many things that look good to you because of how your Judas desires distort your vision. But be assured—if I forbid it," he pointed to the maggots, "that's why."

*****

At the fire, Kailyn watched as the Ruler and Watson finished their conversation over by the bush and returned to the campsite. As they approached, she tossed the piece of toast she had been nibbling into the fire.

"What happened to your appetite, Kailyn?" the Ruler asked.

She sighed. "I don't know. For some reason I just don't feel like eating this morning."

"You don't know because you haven't searched your heart for appetite killers. Think, Kailyn, what is my delicacies?"

Several minutes passed. During those minutes, her clenched jaw gave way to a quivering chin.

"I saw how you hugged Watson, and I was so moved when you told him he was forgiven. But then, for me, you simply touched my wound."

She shook her head. "I know that sounds terrible. I'm grateful for the healing. I am. It's just that … there was no embrace for me. No words of reassurance like you gave Watson. Then this morning you were at Watson's side, teaching him. I feel like I'm on the outside—like you don't …" She buried her face in her hands.

The Ruler knelt next to her and put his arm around her. "You're right. For you, I healed your wound. For Watson, I not only healed him, but I came close to him and made him feel my love and forgiveness."

"But why? Are you displeased with me?"

"No. It is *you* who are displeased with *me*."

She lifted her head, eyes wide.

The Ruler moved around in front of her and took hold of both her hands. "I gave both you and Watson exactly what you sought. You wanted healing, so I healed you. Watson longed for closeness with me, so that is what he received."

He paused for a moment and a steady breeze blew across Kailyn's face. "Do you feel it?"

She inhaled the sweet-smelling draft. “Feels like it’s blowing right through me.”

“You know that *every day* I give you more gifts than you could ever ask for, right? I always will. But there is one thing you can only have as much as you seek—intimacy. It is not possible to have a closer relationship with someone than you seek. You can have as much closeness with me and my Father as you want, but you will find it only in the measure that you pursue it.”

The Ruler’s words stung and soothed at the same time. They exposed her lukewarm attitude about closeness with him but did so in the form of an invitation. Instead of shaming her, the Ruler pointed her to open doors of closeness with him.

She could see now that trying to rescue Abigail while being distant from the Ruler would be pointless. How could she restore Abigail to a state she herself had abandoned?

“So … what do you want us to do now? Is it too late for Abigail?”

“That is not for you to know. Too late or not, yours is to try. As long as she shows any sign at all of being receptive, don’t give up on her. Do what you would want your friends to do if you were in bondage.”

Watson studied the ground and spoke softly. “What if we do … find ourselves in bondage?” He looked up at the Ruler. “When I began this mission, I was prepared to die for you if need be. But then I collapsed at the mildest temptation. And now we must go into the heart of enemy territory and take on the prince and his warriors?"

"You stumbled because you were not alert. Yes, it was a mild test, but even the weakest temptation will defeat you if you drop your guard. You needed this lesson to learn never to underestimate the god of the half-real world again. He will not be content to merely hold Abigail. He is determined to take you captive and use you to carry out his plans. The one he sent yesterday was no insignificant warrior. He is one of the regional powers."

A chill ran through Kailyn. "We faced a regional power?"

"That's right," said the Ruler.

The group sat in silence—until Layth broke it. "We've faced powers before."

"You have," said the Ruler. "And you fought valiantly because, in those battles, you knew they were battles. But in the lowlands, the prince appears as a guardian of light. He knows he can't penetrate your shields, so he lulls you into dropping them."

The Ruler rose and pulled Kailyn to her feet. Watson drew a deep breath, blew it out, and stood with them. Layth looked up at the group, quickly finished the last of his scrambled eggs, and grabbed a handful of bacon from the mound still in the pan. Noticing everyone's eyes on him, he shrugged and said, "For the road."

The Ruler laid his hands on each of the three friends, blessed them, and repeated his commission. "Go. And *stay alert*."

*****

"Anzu failed," Adramelech hissed as he watched Layth, Watson, and Kailyn approaching the orchard.

"They had help," Lucius said. "I'm told they even survived an encounter with the regional power of the canyon lands."

"That would require hundreds of guardians. Either that, or …" Adramelech stroked his chin. "What is the status of the banquet hall server, Charles Baxter?"

"We haven't been able to touch him."

Furrows sunk into Adramelech's brow. His question rolled out in a low growl. "Why … not?"

"The Ruler has assigned six guardians to him. He shouldn't be a problem, though. We have used a sickness in his family, unexpected home repairs, some financial problems, and a legal issue at the banquet hall to take up his time. He is so far behind in his work, and he's so comfortable at home—he won't leave."

"See that he doesn't," Adramelech said, still fuming over the arrival of Watson, Kailyn, and Layth. The strategy of tying Charles down with busyness had worked well in the past, but the margin for error in this operation had just narrowed considerably, and he could not afford another setback.

"If we can keep her isolated," said Adramelech, "Abigail will soon be hardened completely by the deceitfulness of the fruit."

"What about the wind?" Lucius asked.

"If she were walking with the wind, she wouldn't be here. And when someone resists the wind, they almost never turn around without help. That's why it's so important to keep the friends away. I will take care of them myself. You go to Abigail and make sure her faith is destroyed beyond recovery before they get to her."

Lucius looked away.

"You're worried?"

"You just never know with the wind. He's unpredictable."

"There are ways to discern when he blows. Keep a sharp eye on her thoughts and behaviors. Watch for traces of joy and peace … or self-control. And especially love. If any of those symptoms arise, alert me at once."

Chapter 5

"I had forgotten how big it is," Kailyn said quietly as the three friends looked out at endless rows of fruit trees. And this was only one section of the orchard. "Where do we even begin?"

The group walked aimlessly, searching for anything that might give them a clue as to what direction would be best. Progress slowed as the sun rose in the sky. Watson dabbed his face with his sleeve. "Such insufferable heat."

Kailyn squinted at the sun and slapped a mosquito. Her feet ached. She looked at Watson and Layth, who kept walking out ahead of her like she was just some tag-a-long.

On the other hand, at least back here she didn't have to listen to Watson's nonstop chatter. He seemed even more impressed than usual with his own knowledge. And Layth smelled like … well, a man who hadn't bathed in a while.

The hot sun, the insects, the vastness of the orchard—she sighed. *This will never work.*

None of the three friends had any idea they were under attack. Adramelech had worked up a sweat, stimulating selfish attitudes in the three friends—encouraging oversensitivity and fault-finding, sapping patience, and pressing them down with discouragement—all while remaining undetected.

"I think our best chance at finding Abigail will be in the golden city," Kailyn suggested. "Let's start there."

Watson and Layth didn't even slow their pace. "Abigail does not know anyone there," said Watson. "And if she has been eating fruit, she will prefer to be alone. The northwest section of the orchard is the least populated."

Layth agreed, and they continued northward.

Adramelech whispered to Kailyn, *Of course Layth agrees with Watson. You're just a woman. Why would they listen to you?*

The two men had walked thirty feet before noticing Kailyn had stopped. She stood in place, hands on her hips.

When Layth finally glanced over his shoulder, he tapped Watson and motioned toward Kailyn with a tip of his head.

"What are you doing, Kailyn?" Watson asked.

She only shook her head and resumed walking. The men waited for her to catch up, then continued on their course.

Watson responded to her silent objection. "No one in the city is likely to assist us, Kailyn. I am confident the northwest section will be a good place to look."

Kailyn kicked a rock out of her path. *Yeah, like a haystack is a good place to look for a needle.*

She walked in cold silence, mouth still, but mind racing. *Was I out of line? All I did was stop walking for a second. Was that childish? Now I've made everyone uncomfortable. But why don't they at least apologize? Can't they see what they did was hurtful?*

She wondered if the men wrestled with thoughts like hers—alternating between a guilty conscience and self-justification.

The leaves rustled slightly as a subtle breeze touched her cheek. She felt it and she knew what she should do, but hesitated. *Why should I be the one to apologize?*

*****

K-lion, Sol, and Big Red exchanged alarmed glances. They had labored to keep as low a profile as possible, avoiding anything that might attract the attention of warriors in the area. Up to now, they had succeeded. But in the past five minutes all three friends had resisted the wind. Warriors from miles around would hear the clanking of armor falling to the ground. It was like blood in shark-infested waters.

"You know what to do K-lion," Big Red said. "Sol and I will keep watch while you help them. Sol, you go on ahead. I'll guard the flank." The two more seasoned guardians disappeared into the trees in their respective directions as K-lion began his work.

He acted quickly, mixing three of the Ruler's colors in his hands—humility, patience, and love. This very salve had put out the fire of hostility in the Ruler's people on thousands of occasions in the past.

The Wind spoke to him. "Kailyn first."

K-lion knelt beside Kailyn and whispered words of the cottage to open her eyes to the three colors.

Just as her eyes began to open, a voice startled K-lion. "Wandering a little far from the high country, are we?"

K-lion knew that voice. He flashed his gaze upward and his veins ran cold. *Anzu!*

The cold of his fear clashed with the heat of his anger at the sight of the vicious warrior. Thousands of wrecked lives lay in the wake of this savage, merciless being.

Sword sheathed and hands relaxed at his side, a vile grin curled Anzu's tight, thin lips. K-lion sensed the warrior's casual stance was calculated to provoke an attack. But the shrewd guardian knew better. He was powerful in battle, but no match for Anzu.

Big Red, however, might be a different story. If he had seen Anzu coming, he and Sol would be working their way around to flank him.

If just one of the friends wore the armor, none of these warriors would have the boldness to approach. But with all three friends acting in line with their old names, K-lion's only hope was his two comrades.

He shifted his focus to the trees behind Anzu.

"What are you looking for, guardian?" mocked Anzu. "Them?" He pointed as Sol emerged, held by two huge warriors. Then Big Red, surrounded by eight. But none dared lay a hand on him.

K-lion stood and faced his much larger opponent. He had to crane his neck to meet Anzu's gaze with his own defiant glare.

K-lion glanced at Big Red. The ranking guardian lifted his hand slightly and lowered it.

"That's right," Anzu said, "Stand down little guardian. I have to say I'm a bit disappointed. I thought this might be more of a challenge." Anzu strolled around K-lion and Sol, looking them up and down. Then the warriors around Big Red stepped aside to allow Anzu to approach.

Big Red, two hands taller than Anzu, didn't flinch. Anzu spewed his rancid breath inches from Big Red's face. "Who would have guessed the great Chayil would be so easily intimidated? You're not as fearless as the legends paint you when you don't have the advantage, are you, guardian?"

A dozen more warriors stepped out from the surrounding trees and arrayed themselves in a defensive formation. Behind them, the legion commander emerged from the trees. K-lion felt a wave of ice-cold evil.

Adramelech didn't so much as glance at any of the guardians. He fixed his attention on Kailyn, Watson, and Layth like a pacing lion salivating over a piece of raw meat.

With his eyes still on the humans, Adramelech spoke to the guardians. “You will find your work here won’t be as easy as in the high country.”

Several warriors closed in on the friends and drew their swords.

Kailyn turned her head, as if sensing something.

“Stop!” Adramelech commanded. “We must not give away our position. Use the collars.”

The warriors sheathed their swords and stepped back while another warrior approached Kailyn in complete silence. Carefully, quietly, he placed a harness around her neck. The harness held a polished tin plate in front of her face so she could see nothing but herself. He repeated the procedure on Watson and Layth.

*****

Kailyn tried again. “I still think if we just checked the city and—”

“No!” said Watson. “I told you she wouldn’t go to the city.”

“Why don’t you *ever* listen!” she snapped. “You think you know everything, and you won’t even let me finish a sentence!”

“I am fully cognizant of the limitations of my knowledge. And I did listen to you. I simply did not find your argumentation compelling.”

"Why did I even come? I might as well go back home and let you two find her, since you're so sure you know where to look."

When not even Layth responded, something broke inside her. His indifference to her pain hurt even more as she recalled his past tenderness.

It had only been a few months prior that she stood at a precipice on the ridge above the banquet hall, trembling. The memory rushed upon her like it was yesterday.

She had lost her son, then her husband. The outpouring of sympathy from friends at the banquet hall had dissipated and no one really knew what to say to her anymore, so they avoided her. She rarely saw the Ruler at the banquets and wondered if he was avoiding her too.

It was banquet day, and as she looked down at the hall from her perch, even at that distance she heard the sounds of laughter and conversation as everyone joined together at the tables. Did anyone even notice her absence?

Dark impulses whispered in her spirit. *Just let yourself fall. The pain will be over. It's your only escape.* She leaned forward to look down and imagined herself crashing to the rocks below.

Then a huge hand warmed her shoulder and steadied her trembling. Of all the people who might come to encourage her, of course it would be Layth. It was his chief weapon—encouragement. Still, she doubted even he could lift her spirits.

"We've missed you, Kailyn."

She drew a deep breath, afraid that any effort to speak would only unleash a flood of tears.

"Seems like you've lost everything, doesn't it?"

She nodded.

His big arms wrapped around her and held her a long time. She could feel a portion of her sorrow release from her soul into his.

"I feel like there's nothing left for me. I can't imagine ever being happy again."

He drew a strand of her hair from her face and tucked it behind her ear. "Be careful what you say to yourself, Kailyn. Thoughts can strengthen you or destroy you."

"I don't know what to think. Every thought I have is … dark."

"Do you remember when the Ruler told us he is our shepherd, and that even when you pass through the darkest valley, he is with you?"

She lifted her glassy eyes to his.

"The only reason a shepherd leads his flock through a dark valley is to bring them to a better pasture."

Kailyn had never forgotten those words. They had carried her through many dark valleys since that day. As she reminisced, her longing for a strength-giving word from Layth grew. He had been such a good friend in the past. Why was he so cold now?

She caught his gaze. Layth opened his mouth for a brief second, then closed it again and turned away.

*****

Anzu grinned as Layth's deadly javelin clanked to the ground.

Watson offered another defense. "I was not ignoring you. I merely endeavored to identify with Abigail—putting myself in her shoes to get an idea how she might respond to guilt after eating fruit."

"Well, you would know," Kailyn muttered.

One corner of Adramelech's mouth curled upward—the closest he ever came to a smile. *It's working.*

*****

The wind gusted, and stabs of conscience assailed Kailyn. She instantly regretted her crack about Watson's recent failure. All thoughts of Watson's slight and how she had been hurt were forgotten, and she saw only the pain she had inflicted on him with her comment and the harm that was being done by her attitude.

Then she realized how repulsive those evils were in the Ruler's sight, and regret permeated her soul, eclipsing all other feelings.

*****

The warriors stirred when Kailyn snatched the tin, ripped it from the collar, and hurled it away. Anzu dodged it and it slammed against another warrior's head and fell to the ground. Then both Layth and Watson cast aside their tin plates.

Anzu and the other startled warriors stepped back as a fourth guardian, much larger even than Big Red, emerged from the trees on the north side of the clearing. Anzu assessed the intruder and determined he was not one to be trifled with. Big Red, Sol, K-lion, and the newcomer formed a circle, backs to one another, swords drawn.

Anzu moved close to Adramelech. "Who is *that*?"

Adramelech stared at the fearsome guardian. "His name is Gibbor, one of the chief guardians. He watched over King David in ancient times."

A chill went through Anzu when he heard Adramelech mutter to himself, "What is *he* doing here?"

Chapter 6

Anzu drew his sword as the clearing erupted with shouts and clanging weapons. Six additional guardians had rushed the warriors from the surrounding timber in a furious surprise assault. The same moment, the swords of Big Red, Sol, K-lion, and Gibbor exploded on the confused regimen.

Anzu had never seen a guardian move with Gibbor's speed. Ten warriors surrounded him and attacked. He laid waste to all ten with a few effortless strikes.

The six new guardians pushed back the rest of the warriors, allowing Big Red, Sol, and K-lion to rejoin their charges.

K-lion whispered to Kailyn, "Remember the Ruler's words: 'Blessed are the meek. Be patient, tenderhearted, bearing with others in love.'"

What had been a light breeze escalated to a howling wind.

"I'm sorry for what I said, Watson. I don't know where that came from." She bowed her head. "Yes, I do. It came from my arrogant self-importance."

Watson stood in silence.

Kailyn's regret welled up into tears. "Please forgive me. I was wrong."

Watson's surprised expression warmed to a smile. "I, too, apologize. You have much wisdom, Kailyn, and I was a fool to dismiss your ideas. Please forgive me."

Several warriors began to panic when Kailyn and Watson embraced and the selfish, irritable mood the warriors had worked so hard to produce evaporated.

Other warriors stood fast and attempted to entice the three friends to indulge in fruit. Evil thoughts, selfishness, pride, laziness, envy, deceit, greed—every nearby fruit tree, but no temptation took hold. Having walked with the driving gusts the last several moments, the humans desired only real food now.

In a final, desperate attempt, one warrior shook a tree above Kailyn, causing a large, red apple to drop at her feet. With all his might, he tried to entice her. *Just touch it. Press your toe on it to see how firm it is. Prove how much self-control you have. Pick it up then throw it away.*

Kailyn's face turned red, her jaw tightened, and with a powerful swing of her leg she sent the apple into a stone, smashing it to bits.

Layth grinned. "I guess it's true. 'Walk with the wind, and—'"

"And you won't want the fruit!" shouted a voice from behind. The group turned.

"Bax! What are you doing here?" Layth smothered Charles Baxter, the head server at the banquet hall, with an engulfing hug.

"After you left, my conscience bothered me. What kind of shepherd doesn't go after a lost sheep? I kept trying to tell myself, 'It's okay—those three can handle it.' But finally, I realized, Abigail's eternal life is at stake. And the more help the better. So here I am!"

"How did you find us?" Kailyn asked.

"It wasn't hard. I came through the west entrance to the orchard and saw three sets of gigantic tracks in the dirt. The rest was easy."

The warriors retreated to the south like a horde of locusts driven by a hurricane. They covered a mile in a few moments, but Adramelech slowed when an alarming smell reached his nose.

The prince of darkness, red with fury, stood before them. "Hold!"

The warriors stumbled to a halt and all except Adramelech backed away. The prince's stench, which worsened when he was angry, all but disabled the warriors. Adramelech wheezed, eyes burning, as the prince approached.

"My lord, I—"

"You fool!" roared the prince as he seized Adramelech, lifting him off the ground by his neck. "Your idiotic incompetence has jeopardized this whole operation. I should crush your empty skull right now!"

Adramelech clawed at the prince's fingers. "I … thought … if …"

With a flick of his wrist the prince sent the commander flying across the road and slamming into a tree, where he slumped to the ground.

"You thought you could defeat those three with temptations of irritability and discord? Have you learned nothing? You can't take that approach with the humble. They'll repent moments after they fall. And that humility snowballs among the others."

Adramelech struggled to his feet. "Then how—"

"Unbelief! This kind can be defeated only after their faith is weakened." The prince turned to address the warriors. "Their trust in the Ruler is an impenetrable shield. The only hope is to either destroy the shield or convince them to come out from behind it. You must undermine their confidence in the Ruler and the cottage. Only then will they resist the wind. And only when they resist the wind will you have any chance against them."

The prince turned and pointed a gnarled finger at Adramelech. "You have fouled this up enough. I will take over this mission myself. Who's assigned to Abigail?"

Adramelech gestured toward Lucius.

"Approach," the prince demanded.

Lucius stepped forward.

"Status?"

"I believe the hardening is complete. She shows no lingering signs of faith."

*****

The sky dimmed. Kailyn sensed the clouds of judgment gathering on the horizon. Peering into the darkness, she gave voice to the mood of the group. "We have to find her! Soon!"

"I'll go into the city and ask around," Charles said. "You three begin searching here. We can meet up this evening at the west entrance where we came in."

Watson, Layth, and Kailyn combed the orchard, searching for adult-sized tracks. Kailyn searched along the bottom of the ridge, Layth midway up, and Watson along the top.

"Guys! I found something." Kailyn stayed at the edge of the campsite to avoid disturbing it.

Layth arrived first, then Watson. "It's her," Layth said. "Lowlanders don't camp."

Watson examined the fire pit. "Quite recently utilized, it seems."

"Look," Kailyn said, pointing to a set of footprints. "Not quite adult-sized, but bigger than any lowlander prints."

Layth put an arm around Watson and squeezed his shoulder. "She's right," he said with a laugh. "Those ain't lowlander tracks."

With renewed energy, the friends followed the trail. Tracking was easy in the orchard's soft earth.

"The course meanders," Watson said. "That is a good sign. It indicates no specific destination and slow progress. Presumably, we should overtake her before dark."

Minutes later, Watson slowed. Then he stopped, knelt, and traced a footprint with his fingers. His head dropped. Then he looked up at Kailyn. "Tell me it isn't true."

Kailyn had noticed it a few minutes earlier but didn't say anything, hoping it was her imagination. But there was no denying it. Abigail's tracks were shrinking.

"They're still not as small as a lowlander," Layth said. "Maybe she—"

Watson held up a finger and whispered. "Did you hear that?"

Kailyn nodded.

Their gaze bored into the woods in the direction of the sound. Footsteps.

Kailyn spotted her first and went from surprise to delight to shock.

"Abby? Is that you?" Watson said.

What was left of her hair, now gray, hung matted and clumped. And her bloated, deformed body scraped against tree branches as she stumbled through the forest. Vacant eyes receded into her scarred face.

"I heard your voices," Abigail said, expressionless. "What are you doing here?"

"We have come to bring you home," Watson replied. "You are obviously malnourished. If we leave now, we will make the next banquet."

"I can't," came her flat, robotic response. "I'm imprisoned here. I've tried every path. Each one just leads out of one grove into another. There is no way out for me."

Watson drew close and gave her an unrequited embrace. Kailyn smiled at the love of a brother who would not let the smell of his sister's open sores keep him from holding her. Nor did he seem to take offense when Abigail's arms remained at her side.

Releasing the hug, he took her hand. "Come with us."

Abigail acquiesced.

The group started on a direct westward course. Kailyn wanted to ask about Alexander. *Why did she go with him? Was it voluntary? If I ask, will she take it the wrong way?*

"What's the deal with Alexander?" Layth blurted. "Adam said you two were hold'n hands."

Abigail's eyes shot to Kailyn, then dropped to the ground. "I just … couldn't go with Adam. You wouldn't understand. You don't know what it's like for me."

Watson drew close to Abigail as they walked. "Abby, we only want to—"

"I don't want to talk about it."

Watson took her hand and the group closed the distance to the border in silence.

At the boundary line, Abigail stopped as if she had run into an invisible wall.

"Don't stop," Kailyn said. "This is the border. You've made it. Come on."

Abigail appeared almost catatonic and stood motionless. The men took hold of her arms and pulled, but she didn't budge. She might as well have been behind iron bars.

Abigail sighed. "Every attempt to escape has been like this. I told you—it's hopeless. I'm hopeless. Look at me. Look what I've become." She began clawing at her face, drawing blood.

"Abigail! No!" Kailyn cried. Her stomach knotted when she realized the hideous deformities on Abigail's face had been caused by self-harm.

Abigail turned back toward the orchard and began walking.

Watson pleaded with her. "No Abby. Wait."

She stopped but didn't turn. She spoke in a near whisper. "Charles always told me, 'Walk with the wind, and you won't want the fruit.' Now I understand. I resisted the wind, and now my heart is hopelessly enslaved to the fruit. I can't break free."

Layth stepped in front of her. "Take this." He placed a cottage piece into her palm. The lettering on the piece said, "Do not become weary. At the proper time, you will have success if you do not give up. Consider him who endured such opposition, so you will not grow weary and lose heart. In your struggle, you have not yet resisted to the point of shedding your blood. And you have forgotten that you are his daughter."

Abigail held the piece for several moments, trembling. Then it slipped from her grasp and disappeared in the dirt at her feet. "If the Ruler wants me free, why doesn't he give me the strength to leave? I've tried and tried. I just … can't."

With that remark, Kailyn thought she heard a hint of life in Abigail's voice. *Maybe there is something left in her soul.*

Layth placed a second cottage piece in Abigail's hand. He closed her fingers around it, then wrapped his hand around hers so she couldn't drop it. "You can do all things through the Ruler who strengthens you. Your temptations are common ones, and the Ruler will never let you be tested beyond what you can bear but will always provide a way out so you can stand up under it."

"You don't understand," she said. "I have searched everywhere for the way out. I've pleaded with the Ruler to help me."

Layth took Abigail's other hand in his and stooped to catch her downward gaze. "Don't just plead. *Trust.*"

"Yes," Kailyn added. "If he promised to make a way out, he'll make a way out. You must believe that because if you're not ready when that way out comes, you'll miss it."

"I'm afraid I already have." Abigail's lips quivered and a trace of color returned to her face. "You saw it with your own eyes when you tried to pull me out. Not even you are powerful enough to free me."

"Of course we're not. But this is." Layth turned to Watson and nodded. Watson stepped forward and presented her with a large piece of cottage wood in the shape of a sword. "The Ruler instructed us to give you this weapon when you were ready to take it. It has freed thousands before you."

Abigail took hold of the heavy piece, both hands on the handle, dragging the tip in the dirt. Her awkward effort to swing it didn't so much as lift the tip from the ground.

Kailyn and Watson exchanged a confused glance, then stepped forward to help her. With their assistance, the sword rose slightly, then dropped when they let go.

Kailyn frowned. *It shouldn't be that hard. Something's wrong.*

Chapter 7

It was late afternoon when Charles arrived at the rendezvous point. "We found her!" Kailyn called as she saw their beloved server approaching.

Charles ran the rest of the way and gave Abigail a long embrace—without any sign that he even noticed her deformities.

When they had debriefed him on all that had happened, Charles put his arm around Abigail again. "We'll get you out of here. Don't lose hope."

Abigail closed her eyes and laid her head on his shoulder.

"You're tired," Kailyn said. "Why don't you get some sleep. We'll keep watch through the night."

As Abigail slept, the others sat around a fire and discussed their next steps.

"Why isn't this working?" Kailyn asked. "The sword is from the cottage. It should give her power."

Charles' grandfatherly smile eased her anxiety. He always knew what to do.

He pointed to the woodpile by the fire. “Layth, hand me that stick, the one shaped like a club. Yes, that one.”

Layth tossed it across the fire and Charles stood to catch it. He approached a large maple, took aim, and swung the heavy club with both hands at a branch.

The branch shook slightly as the club bounced back toward Charles. He looked at Kailyn. “Healthy tree, right?”

Then he turned to another maple and repeated the assault on a like-sized branch. This time the branch snapped off, barely slowing the club’s motion.

Charles tossed the club back to Layth and faced Kailyn. “Why did the second one break?”

“Because that tree is dead,” she said.

“Not quite,” he replied, pointing to a section of branches that still had green leaves. He backed up a step to take in the entire tree, arms folded. “Traces of life in spots, but you’re right. It’s clearly on its way out.”

He stripped a handful of leaves from the first tree and returned to the dying tree. “It just needs some green, right?” He placed them on a branch and watched as they slid off and fell to the ground.

Kailyn chuckled. “I don’t think that’s how it works, Charles.”

Charles feigned a look of surprise. “You’re saying I can’t fix the problem with external changes?”

Watson approached the tree and ran a hand down the trunk. He peeled off a section of bark. “It is diseased. To discover the cause would require felling the thing and examining its rings." He pointed to the ground. "The roots as well."

"Somethin's wrong in Abigail's heart," Layth said. "Is that what you're sayin' Bax?"

"Ah, yes, of course," said Watson. "We endeavored to alter the direction of Abigail's feet, but the feet cannot traverse long in a direction opposite that of the heart."

"Makes sense," Kailyn said. "But then how do we help her? How do we diagnose what's wrong in her heart?"

"The heart is a world of complexity," Charles said. "We would need to ask her what inclinations led her to make the decisions she made. What were her motives? What feelings led to her being vulnerable? What thought patterns produced those feelings? What perspectives did she have that led to evil reactions? What attitudes or desires caused her to look at things from those perspectives, and what caused those attitudes? What is her heart in love with that it should hate or apathetic about that it should love? What is she hoping in? What is she trusting in? What wrong beliefs underlie all this? And what—"

"I get the idea," Kailyn said. "But figuring all that out will take forever. What about in the meantime? Isn't there something we could do now?"

"There is. To sort all that out, she's going to need some breathing room. Right now, she's assaulted with constant temptations from every direction. We need to clear a perimeter so she can have a break from the onslaught of temptation."

Work began early the next morning. It wasn't long before a small crowd of lowlanders gathered to see this strange group of children and their little axes. The people shook their heads as the kids felled one fruit tree after another and tore grapevines and berry bushes out by the roots.

With her deformities, Abigail couldn't swing an ax. But Charles put her to work clearing small twigs which, for her, proved hard work. "Temptation is strongest in times of idleness and boredom," he explained, "and evil desire grows in the garden of leisure. Keeping busy with good work will leave little time to wander into the enemy's traps."

The efforts seemed to be working. With each passing day, Abigail ate less and less fruit.

*****

Anzu fumed. "Shouldn't we be doing something? We're losing her."

The prince, who had only one eyebrow, raised it. Anzu knew the prince was not accustomed to being second-guessed. If a consequence followed, so be it. But something needed to be said. All his hard work was being squandered.

Fury rose within Anzu as the prince belittled him with a condescending look—like a person deciding whether a fly was worth swatting.

Finally, the prince looked away with a scoff. "You think we're losing her because you're an even greater fool than she is. You don't understand what keeps her in bondage." The prince clenched his fists. "My grip on her is stronger now than it has ever been. The false hope she is gaining from her reduced indulgence only doubles the strength of her chains."

He turned and pointed to Abigail. "Look for yourself—not at her hands or feet, but her heart."

Heavy irons bound her entire inner being—will, motives, affections, attitudes—all of it.

"I'm not worried about her. She's mine. The only question now is how many of her friends I can take down. I need them out of the way for the next stage of my plan."

*****

Guardians lined the halls of the cottage, from the foyer to the throne room. All were heavily armed, expressionless, and silent. Only the echoing steps of the unwelcome visitor interrupted the quiet. Each guardian closed in behind him as he passed, blocking his retreat.

That suited the prince of darkness just fine. The Father had granted his request for an audience, and no intimidation by the guardians would deter him.

The prince entered the throne room with his head bowed, knowing that a glimpse in the wrong direction would be his last. He grimaced with hatred as he dropped involuntarily to his knees before the throne.

The chief guardian stepped from the Father's side. "Your request," he thundered. It was not a question.

The Father's normally loving eyes burned white with judgment.

"You have not permitted me to touch Abigail," the prince began. "But she willingly came to me. She has forgotten you. You mean so little to her that a single grape has a greater tug on her heart than your son's table. Her 'repentance' is half-hearted. And by your own word, the Ruler's sacrifice can't apply to her because she no longer shows any sign of faith."

"My request is simple. It is time to conclude the process." His next words came out as a growl meant to send shivers down the spines of the guardians. "Allow me to devour her."

Many of the guardians were visibly shaken. It wasn't that long ago the prince had knelt in this very spot requesting the same thing for Alexander. The gasps among the guardians were audible that day when the chief guardian delivered the Father's answer: "Permission granted." Would he now give Abigail over as well?

*****

Abigail steadied herself. *What was that?*

There it was again. The ground … moved.

"Hey, I think I felt a little trem …" Crack! A huge limb above them broke off. The same instant, Abigail tumbled to the side—shoved by Layth who took the force of the falling branch. The limb flayed his leg open.

The ground convulsed. Trees crashed down all around them. Even at this distance, Abigail heard the rumble of buildings collapsing in the city.

Lowlanders scattered like frenzied ants seeking safety, but there was nowhere to hide. Shouts arose. "It's the judgment! The Ruler has come!"

Abigail wanted to scream. *No! I'm not ready.*

Cries rang out from every direction as people were crushed by falling trees or swallowed alive by the earth as massive fissures cracked open. The injured screamed in pain and cursed Ruler. There was no escape. No refuge. Nowhere to run.

When the shaking ended, Abigail surveyed the devastation. "Layth! Kailyn! Watson!" *Where are they?*

A woman shouted. "She's one of them!"

Abigail turned to find a group of enraged lowlanders approaching.

"You brought this upon us!"

"This happened because of you mountain people and all your hateful speech about the orchard!"

A man shouted, "Here's a message for your Ruler …" and shoved Abigail to the ground.

That ignited the crowd. They closed around her and beat her mercilessly. She curled into a ball with her arms protecting her face, but the kicks and punches landed all over her body. Two men dragged her around by her hair.

"Please, I—" a kick to her ribs took her breath away. Then another blow to her face.

Then, the beating stopped. She still heard shouting but dared not uncover her face.

"Abigail, run!"

It's Watson! She looked up. Watson had pulled two of the men away from her onto their backs, and the crowd turned on him. "Run!" he shouted again.

She stood on rubber legs and stumbled forward. The world spun. Screaming agony met her every step, but she didn't care. She had to escape.

In a few short moments, shouts closed in behind her—the angry crowd gaining quickly. Her disfigured and battered body couldn't obey the commands from her mind. It was like running in a dream—slogging through molasses.

She stumbled, kept her feet, tripped again, and fell. Her head pounded. Her vision blurred. She struggled back to her feet and pushed her body to new limits. But not even adrenaline could overcome her weakness. They would soon be upon her.

"Help me!" she shrieked, desperately scanning the landscape for her friends. Just ahead she saw a thick grove of trees where she might be able to hide—if she could make it.

To her left, a man angled up the hill toward her. She looked again at the trees ahead. Another man emerged from those trees, also running toward her.

The man on the hillside called her name, "Abigail, come this way!"

Layth!

Before she could take a step toward him, she heard her name again. "This way, Abigail!" She turned and slowed. It was Alexander.

Only a moment to decide as the crowd charged. Layth was a powerful man, but his strength lay mostly in spiritual matters. This was a physical fight, and Alexander was twice Layth's height and three times as thick. She ran toward Alexander.

"No!" shouted Layth. "Down here!" But she had already committed.

Layth changed course. *He's headed for the crowd!* A lump formed in her throat as she realized he was going to meet them head-on to give her a chance to make the trees.

When she reached Alexander, he pointed south. "This way." He scooped her into his arms and carried her all the way to the southern boundary of the orchard.

"There is a place here where you can be safe." He made his way down a small ridge, arcing around some downed timber.

When he reached the bottom, he set her down. "There," he said, pointing to a cave. "No one knows about this place. Hide in that cave and you'll be safe."

Abigail crouched to see inside, but it was too dark.

"What's in there?"

"Don't worry. I know it looks scary, but trust me—it's safe. Once you get inside, it opens into a wide space. I'll come back soon with a lamp and supplies."

Abigail crept toward the mouth of the cave. She sat, scooted close to the opening, and extended her leg, waving it side to side to feel what was inside. She stretched downward to feel where she could step. Nothing. She pulled back, turning toward Alexander. "I don't feel any—"

His great hands shoved her into the cave and she plummeted into complete darkness. Her body impacted the angled side, stopping her momentarily. But then she began sliding, scraping along the rocky wall. She groped for a hold, but the incline was too steep.

As she picked up speed, she flailed. Finally, her hand met something hard—the other side of the cave. The walls continued to close as she slid downward. The funnel soon became too narrow for her body and she came to a painful stop, wedged at her hips, legs dangling. She tried pushing against the sides to lift herself, but the smooth walls gave no traction.

Judging from the circle of light above, she guessed she had dropped thirty feet. Mustering her remaining strength, she called out, "Alexander! Help me!"

His giant head appeared in the opening. "Why ask me for help?" His voice dripped with venom. "Call for your Ruler. You think he's so powerful and loving—see if he saves you."

She looked up in disbelief. Was he so embittered that he would murder her just to strike out at the Ruler? She clawed at the sides but remained hopelessly wedged.

She heard a grunt from above. Pebbles trickled down on her. Then a boulder rolled into the opening above. The circle of light went black. The boulder dropped through the opening and rained down more dirt as it plummeted toward her. She pulled her arms over her head as she prepared to be crushed, but the boulder wedged just a few feet above her head, sealing her subterranean tomb.

Looking up into the darkness, she heard her own screams die in the sealed chamber.

She tried to control her panic but without success. Thrashing and flailing, she only wedged herself more and more tightly until exhaustion finally stilled her.

Her screams turned to sobs. Later, sobs became moans. Finally, drained of life, her body refused to draw another breath. Her eyes fell closed.

Her burning lungs screamed for air and forced another effort to snatch one final taste of precious oxygen. But no sooner did the first wisp of air enter, than her exhausted chest released it back into the dark void.

Each gasp seemed to claim her final wisp of strength.

Alexander's words cut deep. *What* would *happen if I called to the Ruler?*

She had been defying him ever since she came to the lowlands. The Great Wind had stopped blowing on her long ago. She had made her choice and was now getting exactly what she deserved.

In her thoughts of the Ruler, she could only imagine him as angry, yet she desired to see him. Even if she was to be condemned, she wanted another glimpse of his colors. As her life ebbed away, all empty desires—including her desire for life itself—detached from her, like rotten apples dropping from a branch. Her whole existence resolved around one central craving—to see the Ruler.

Out of the dark silence the Mighty Wind spoke. "I gave you a loving family. I gave you greater joy than anyone in the high country. I gave you your beauty and your smile. I gave you life, and—"

Her mind filled in the rest. *I gave you all those gifts, and this is the thanks I get? You ignore me and eat fruit?*

But that's not what he said. His next words jarred her soul.

" … I gave you all that, and if that had been too little, I would have given you even more."

Did she hear that right? *I would have given you even more*?

"My Lord, how can that be? I don't deserve … are you saying you will always keep giving until there is enough to satisfy me?"

"Always. But only if you look to me alone to fill you. The orchard can fill your mouth, but only I can promise to *satisfy*."

Abigail remembered the plaque above the kitchen doors at the banquet hall. It had been her favorite title for the Father—and the longest. *He who gives generously to all without finding fault.*

Then two of the Mighty Wind's words leapt back into her mind with a jolt. *Would have.* He *would have* given her more. Her heart ached with renewed stabs of remorse. How much of the Father's life had she forfeited?

All this time I've been starving in misery in the lowlands, I could have been feasting. My joy, my smile, Watson, my friends—all lost. And for what? A stupid grape that makes me sick.

The pain of regret was worse than the pain of death.

Then, the ache from her injuries softened. Her thoughts clouded. Consciousness slipped away.

*****

After the earthquake, most of the lowlanders returned to the city. Kailyn ran to where she had last seen Charles. The carnage she had witnessed haunted her. The lifeless, mangled body of an elderly man crushed by a tree had imprinted itself on her memory. The man reminded her of Charles, and the thought of what may have happened to him … She cried out. "Charles!"

"I'm up here!"

Her heart leaped. She scampered up the hillside and threw her arms around him.

"Are you okay?" they both asked at once.

"I have some bruises," Kailyn said, "but nothing serious. Have you seen the others?"

Charles pointed to the south. “Here come Layth and Watson now.”

Kailyn greeted the men with the brightest smile she had mustered in quite a while. “I’m so glad you’re all right!”

Neither of the men returned her smile.

Kailyn’s faded as well. “What’s wrong?” Her mind raced, finally landing on the one thing she didn’t want to consider. “Is it Abigail? Is she …”

Watson shook his head slowly and closed his eyes.

“She was … buried,” said Layth.

Kailyn staggered backward and sat down on a stone, unable to speak—barely able to breathe.

Why? The Ruler knows everything. Why did he even send us here if he knew we would fail?

It was a war, and wars have casualties. She understood that. Still, the pain knifed her to the core.

Paralyzed with grief, none of the friends wanted to begin the long journey home. They agreed they would set up camp, stay the night, and set out for home in the morning.

Chapter 8

Abigail came to with a start when something touched her foot. She reflexively jerked, smashing her knee against the rocky side. Something gripped her other leg. She kicked but couldn't break free. Now it had both legs. It pulled her downward. Was she about to be eaten by some hideous underground creature?

The thing had an iron grip and pulled harder and harder. She thought her hips would break as they were forced through the tiny opening. Finally, her body squeezed through and fell, landing on the creature.

She scrambled through the dirt on hands and knees to get away and realized she could see. A lamp illuminated the cavern. When she spun to face the creature, her heart jumped. She sprang to her feet and ran to the man she thought she would never see again. His generous smile was visible only for a moment before he wrapped her up in his strong arms.

"Adam! Oh, Adam! I thought I was going to die."

For a moment, all was well in his arms. But when he began to release her, she gripped tighter. She didn't want him to see her hideous face.

She held him tight as she spoke. "What has become of the city? Was it destroyed in the judgment?"

"That wasn't the judgment. The prince of darkness caused the earthquake. It was to turn the people against us."

As her adrenaline receded, so did her strength. Her legs gave way, and Adam lowered her gently to the ground.

He pulled a vial from his jacket, removed the lid, and tipped a drop onto his finger. He touched his finger to her lips and she tasted the drop.

Strength returned. The pain remained, but refreshment washed through her soul. Energy infused her body and she felt she could stand—even run if she had to.

"How did you find me?" she said, still not able to look him in the eye.

"The Ruler sent me to join the others. When I found Layth, he showed me where Alexander buried you. I started to tell Layth about these tunnels, but some lowlanders showed up and we got separated."

"You've been down here before?"

"Lots of times. Years ago, when I was searching for the pond that brought me into this world, I stumbled across these tunnels. Since there was no pond anywhere above ground, I began searching down here.

I drew maps of the whole maze of these tunnels, so I know them pretty well. When Layth showed me where you went down, I wasn't sure if I'd be able to find this exact spot but … here I am. I think a guardian may have helped me."

Abigail finally looked him in the eye. "So … you met the Ruler? At the banquet hall?"

His eyes lit up. "Yes! And this time I could taste the food! Not all of it, but enough. It was amazing. Everything you told me was true."

She nodded. "You could taste it because you escaped from the orchard." Her words pressed even more weight of condemnation on her soul. Her shoulders slumped. "I don't have the willpower you have."

He shook his head. "It wasn't just because I left the orchard. Do you remember the first time I came to the banquet? I had left the orchard and the fruit, but still, I couldn't taste the food. This time I could. One of the servers explained it to me."

She cocked her head.

"He showed me the lack of taste had been because of my longing for you. Not that it was wrong for me to desire you, but the way I was doing it made it just like a desire for fruit because I cared more about being with you than I did about the banquet. The banquet food becomes tasteless when there's any rival desire. That's why I couldn't taste it."

"So my efforts to bring you to the banquet turned out to be the very thing that kept you from tasting it?"

Renewed self-loathing overtook her and she began to claw at her face. But Adam took her hand in his and pulled her head to his chest.

For a moment, her anxieties melted into his body from hers. She felt at home in his arms. In the silence of the cave she heard only the rhythm of his heartbeat, and it soothed her. Something strong pulsed within Adam's chest. Something … *new*.

She stepped back. "You went through the cottage!"

He smiled. "How did you know?"

She laid her hand on his chest. "I can tell you're different. You …" Then her face darkened and she turned away. "Let me guess. Your first mission was to come and convince me to leave the orchard."

"No, not to convince you. The Ruler knows you are already convinced. My mission is to show you what holds you here."

She faced him again, eyes wide. "Tell me! Others come and go at will. Why can't I?"

"There is a plaque in the wisdom room that says, 'The desires of the unfaithful imprison them.' Abigail, nothing holds you here but the chains of your own desires."

"How could that be? I want nothing more than to leave. I hate this place. I don't even like the fruit that much anymore."

He gave a knowing nod. "Your desires for the fruit may be small, but they are still the strongest desires you have. To break free, you must be drawn away from the orchard by a stronger desire."

"I don't think my desire to escape from the orchard could be any stronger."

"That's just it. You want to escape *from* the orchard. But the power to change your heart comes from the place you want to escape *to*. Without the power of allure, escape is impossible."

A tear trickled down her cheek. "No matter which direction I went, there was only headwind. Even when I turned around, it was never at my back."

"It was never at your back because you were never running *toward* the Ruler. Only *away from* the orchard."

Adam reached into his shirt and pulled up a cottage piece that hung from a string around his neck.

"Do you remember this?"

She nodded slowly, then reached to touch the piece. She turned it to read the inscription, though she knew what it said. *The banquet is like a treasure hidden in a field. A man finds it and, in his joy, trades all he has for the field.*

"You gave me this before I had ever been to the banquet. But it's not just for those who have never been. It's for you, right now. You're trapped here because your heart has lost sight of the value of the treasure."

"The treasure is the Ruler." Her face grew hot. "You're saying … you're accusing me of not valuing the Ruler?" She stepped back from him. "I'm the one who showed you that treasure, Adam. If I didn't think he was a treasure, why would I be trying so hard to turn my back on the fruit?"

"Of course you think he's a treasure. You *know* he's a treasure. But the problem isn't one of thinking or knowing. It's in *valuing*.

We all do things we know we shouldn't do every day—choosing things of lesser value over what we know to be of greater value. We don't choose the greater things until we not only *know* them to be better, but also *feel* that they're better."

She stared at him a few seconds, then shook her head. Arms folded, she asked, "What do you mean, 'feel they're better'?"

Adam stepped close. "You told me the reason you're stuck is lack of willpower. That's not true. You have all the willpower you need. What if someone had a knife to Kailyn's throat and said, 'If you eat that grape, I will kill your friend.' You would have plenty of willpower to resist the grape. It's not about your willpower—it's about what you value. Saving Kailyn would *feel* valuable enough to you to surpass your desire for the grape. Valuing is a function of both what you think and how you feel."

Abigail paced, raking her fingers through her hair. Then she turned her back to Adam and spoke softly. "I have had good times with friends in the banquet hall, but the cottage itself has no tug on my heart anymore. I know it should. I know I should want to be near the Ruler more than I want anything else, but when I think about being in the cottage, it doesn't feel like anything there could match the pleasures I have here. I know that isn't true, but it's how I feel."

Adam touched her shoulder and she turned to face him. He wiped a tear from her cheek. "That's why I'm here."

She looked at him with pleading eyes. "How do I change my desires? How can I change how things seem or feel?"

"Do you remember the happiness room?"

She nodded. "The Ruler took me there not long after I first met him. But to be totally honest, I don't remember being happy in that room. I haven't gone back to it very often because whenever I go, I come out just as unhappy as when I went in."

Adam smiled. "The Ruler sent me here to show you how—"

Adam and Abigail both jumped at a sound from the tunnel behind Abigail. Adam put his finger to his lips and extinguished the lamp.

The cave fell into suffocating darkness. Abigail thought she knew what complete blackness was, but the darkness in this place ... She began to shake.

Something touched her! She jumped and strained to suppress a scream. Her heart pounded so hard she felt it in her head.

"Shhhh," Adam whispered. "It's me. We have to move." Taking her hand, he guided her forward.

After ten or twelve careful steps, the sound of their footfalls changed. Had they entered a tunnel? Adam's pace quickened.

A minute later she thought she heard another sound behind them. Adam must have heard it too because he stopped moving. They both held their breath.

There it was again! She squeezed Adam's hand with strength she didn't know she had.

Adam's whisper, barely audible, was so close she felt his breath on her ear. "It's following us. You stay right here. I'm going back to find out what it is."

"Wait. You're going … back there?"

"I don't like not knowing what's behind me."

She grasped for his arm, but he was already gone. His footsteps echoed back the way they had come. Then, silence.

She stood motionless for a long moment, peering into the darkness ahead, then behind. *What if something …?* She pressed herself against the side of the tunnel, one arm flat against the wall, the other felt open space—a diagonal crack in the wall.

She squeezed inside. A pointed stone gouged her thigh. She pressed into a pushup position to relieve the pressure. As she waited, she alternated between the pain of the rock and the fatigue in her arms.

Minutes felt like hours. The thick darkness pressed down on her like a smothering blanket. If Adam were gone much longer, she feared she would lose her sanity. She resolved to think warm, happy thoughts, but no matter how hard she tried, nothing warm or happy would come to mind.

A long time passed. Too long. *What happened to him?* Shivering in the cold, she began to face the possibility that Adam had been captured or eaten or whatever happened to people in the secret lowlands' underground. *How long should I wait? I can't stay here forever.*

Ten different times she decided to leave her hiding place to find a way out. And ten times she moved no more than an inch before fear changed her mind. The dangers of the cave were too great. She would remain in her miserable haven.

Her thoughts returned to what Adam had said—trapped by her own desires. *Stupid Judas desires!* She found herself hating her own heart.

She squinted right—opposite the direction Adam had gone. Did she see a glimmer? Or were her eyes playing tricks on her in the maddening darkness? She looked the other direction, then back again. *Yes, something's there.* Calling it "light" would be going too far. But the darkness didn't seem as heavy down that way.

She tried to climb out of her torturous refuge but could hardly move. Strength had left her arms, and her leg had gone numb.

She tried again. Pushing with her good leg and twisting her torso, she finally worked her way free and fell to the cave floor.

Chapter 9

A light burned Abigail's eyes. She pressed them closed and covered her face but still saw it. And it was getting brighter.

"Abigail!"

"Adam? Is that you?"

When her eyes adjusted, she saw Adam moving toward her, lantern in hand.

Seeing her on the ground, he ran to her. He knelt and pulled her to a sitting position. "Are you okay? What happened?"

Pent-up tears of fear broke free and comingled with sobs of relief as Adam held her.

When the tears had done their work and feeling returned to her leg, she let go of Adam and stood. Blood ran from her hands, but it wasn't hers. The lantern's light revealed lacerations on Adam's arms, neck, and face.

"Oh, Adam. What happened?"

"I'm fine. There are some ornery critters down here. But that one—let's just say he won't be bothering anyone ever again."

"When you left, didn't you go back that way?" She pointed. "How did you get—"

"All these tunnels connect. But don't worry. I know the way to the surface."

She grasped his arm. "Take me out of here."

Adam's decisiveness at each fork in the tunnels gave Abigail comfort. He knew where he was going. "Where will we come out? Can we take these tunnels all the way out of the orchard?"

"I'm afraid not. We'll have to pass through the orchard above ground."

She slowed. Hope drained from her like water from a sieve. "Adam, when I see the fruit, I … lose control. Sometimes I even …" She took his arm. "I don't think I can do it."

Adam stopped, set the lantern on the ground, and took her face in both hands. "You *can* do it. The Ruler promised. And no matter how many times you stumble, I won't leave you. My mission is to present you to the Ruler safe and sound, and I will die before leaving this place without you."

She laid her head against his hand and closed her eyes. Her soul soaked in his confident, reassuring tone like a dry, withering plant taking in a gentle rain.

She opened her eyes and looked up at him. "I keep thinking about what you said before about desires and what my heart values. I try to tell myself that the banquet is the ultimate treasure, but nothing changes."

"It doesn't have to be the exuberant delight you had before. You said yourself that your desires for the fruit are weak. All you need is desire for the banquet that is slightly stronger than that. That's all it will take to break the chains. Once you're free, then we can work on the next steps."

Her skin cooled, raising goosebumps. *What was that?* She hadn't felt that sensation since ... *Did I just imagine that?*

There it is again. This time her hair moved ever so slightly. *The breeze!*

Adam's words were beginning to make sense. She thought of her hiding place in the cave. It was a horrible place, yet she had chosen to remain in it. Miserable as it was, she stayed because there was no other option she desired more. That crevice was like the orchard—a miserable haven she couldn't leave because as weak as her desires for fruit were, her desires for real food were weaker still.

"If my desire for the Ruler and his banquet is so weak that it isn't enough to free me from this place, how do I change that?"

"The only place desires change is in the happiness room. The Ruler told me of your experiences in that room and sent me to show you why it didn't work for you."

She gave him a sideways look. "I'm listening."

The lantern flickered. Adam trimmed it, picked it up, and resumed walking.

"The Ruler took me to the happiness room right after my second visit to the mirror room. I could hardly keep up with him in the hallway. He was so excited. But when we got to the door, he said, 'You wait out here' and then went inside."

"He did that with me too," she said. "I finally went in, but he wasn't there. I looked around for a while, then left. When you went in, did you see him?"

"Not at first. But I knew he had to be in there somewhere, so I kept searching. It's a huge room—the biggest in the whole cottage. Several times I thought I had searched every possible place and felt like giving up, but I wanted so badly to find him, I looked some more. Each time that happened, I discovered a new area I hadn't yet searched."

"So did you find him?"

"Yes! One of the times I was about to give up, out of the corner of my eye I saw two of his colors shining on a wall. My heart raced. I couldn't tell at first where the colors were coming from, but I knew he had to be near. So I called out. There was no response, but I kept calling, louder and louder. Before long, I was shouting at the top of my lungs until he finally answered."

Abigail listened, transfixed. "What did he say?"

"He told me to sit down and watch the colors. So I did. For a long time, I sat and watched them move along the wall. The longer I watched, the more colors I saw."

"And that gave you happiness?"

"Not really. I very much enjoyed watching them, but that isn't what gave me happiness."

She stopped walking and grabbed his arm. "How did you get it?"

"Just listen," he said with a wink, reminding her of when she had said that to him.

He resumed walking. "After I had watched for some time, the Ruler told me to get up and go over to the wall. So I did. Then he said, 'Reach out your hand, and touch one of the colors.'"

Abigail caught her breath. "You *touched* them? What was that like?"

"I can't even describe the happiness I felt. It was unlike anything I …" a broad smile cut off his words. "It had never occurred to me I could actually touch the colors, but they are more than just refractions of light. They have substance. In fact, they're more substantial than anything else in the world. I could touch them, pull them around me like a robe, even climb inside them. The more contact I had with them, the more intense the effects became."

"Effects? You mean happiness?"

"Definitely happiness. But more than that. What I experienced was better than life itself. Better than all the best things in life. They strengthened me. While I touched them, I thought … no, I *knew* I could go through the worst imaginable suffering without losing my joy. I felt courage. I understood things that never made sense before. I was full of hope, full of love, my soul was at peace, and most of all, my Judas desires weakened and my good desires became overpowering—especially my desire to be near the Ruler."

Tears now streaked Abigail's face. She felt as if she were in that room touching the colors herself. And, in fact, she was. At least two of the Ruler's colors caressed her—his love, which she experienced through this man the Ruler had sent to help her, and his wisdom, which illuminated her soul as Adam spoke.

She took a moment to enjoy touching these two colors, basking in pleasure. Joy trickled into her heart and strength into her bones.

The sensation sparked memories of past banquets—times when the Ruler emerged from the kitchen and sat next to her and ate with her. Times of loneliness when he found her in a secluded place and listened as she poured out her thoughts. Moments when he escorted her through room after room in his cottage, overwhelming her with wonder. Gratitude stirred her affections as she remembered.

"I wish I could go back to the way things were," she said wistfully.

"No," Adam said. "Not back. Forward. One thing I learned in the promise room—his colors are new every morning. He never runs out of ideas. What he has in store for you will dwarf even the best of what you knew in the past."

Hope poured into Abigail's soul. A river of joy rose within her, fed by the three tributaries of gratitude from past experiences with the Ruler, hope of future encounters, and delight in her enjoyment of his colors in the present. And as joy rose, her strongest desires shifted from the fruit to the Ruler's banquet.

*****

Lucius stared at his empty hand. His cold, rigid fingers still curled in the shape of a heart that was no longer there. *I had her!*

He stumbled, reeling from the shock of loss and disbelief. Abigail stood shimmering before him like the haze of a dream. He reached for her, but the river of joy that washed her from his grasp held him at its banks. He cursed the wind.

Chapter 10

"Adam, I can feel the chains dropping from my heart. I'm free!"

"You are unchained," he said, "which makes escape possible. But we still have to make it out of the orchard. And that won't be easy. The prince will do everything he can to recapture us both before we make it out."

Abigail considered the journey. They would have to pass through thousands of fruit trees between the cave and the clearing—a gauntlet. Suddenly she felt like a wounded soldier a hundred miles behind enemy lines.

Adam drew a wooden sword from the scabbard on his belt. Holding it flat across his palms, he presented it to her. "With this, you will be able to fight your way through."

Abigail frowned at the weapon.

"What's wrong?" Adam asked

"I know that sword. It's the one the others gave me before. It didn't help. I couldn't even lift it."

"Yes, it's heavy. That's what makes it so powerful. One hard swing, and nothing can withstand the blow."

"I don't doubt it. But what good is that if I can't swing it? Look at you—even with all your muscles, you need two hands just to raise it."

Adam smiled. "You'll be able to wield it when the time comes."

Then he looked down at the sword and his mouth tightened, like a man concealing some unspeakable secret.

After a pause, he spoke pensively, as if talking to himself. "Swinging it isn't the hardest part. It's at the moment of decision, when you see the one against whom you must raise this sword—in that instant, will you hesitate?" He seemed to be on the verge of tears, as if reliving a dreadful memory.

He returned the sword to its scabbard. "Forget the sword for now. When we reach the others, I'll show you how to get the strength you need to swing it. But first I need to get you to the clearing. We're going to have to pass through some of the densest portions of the orchard, and—"

Abigail stopped. "Adam, I … I can't. I know what happens when fruit is within reach. I'll lose control." She turned her face away. "I can't go out there."

"What you can't do is stay here. You'll be devoured in this cave." He took her hands in his. "I'll help you. If it costs me my life, I *will* get you back to the Ruler."

She drew a deep breath and followed Adam. Ten minutes passed in silence as she contemplated the upcoming test.

The lantern flickered. "It's almost out," she said. "Do you have more oil?"

"No, but it doesn't matter. We're close. There should be an opening around the next corner." He spoke with a hint of questioning in his tone. "Strange. I would expect to see some daylight by now."

Passing the bend, they stopped. "Oh, no!" Abigail said. "Now what?"

What looked like a stone wall sealed the cave opening from the outside. Not even a glimmer of light penetrated.

"No one could move a boulder that size," Adam said. "Not even the little ones. It must have fallen in the earthquake."

Her stomach churned as the beginnings of panic threatened yet again. She grasped Adam's arm. "Is there another way out?"

He held up the dimming lantern. "Not that we could reach before losing our light."

He paused.

"Here, hold this," he said, handing her the lamp. "You were wondering about the sword?"

He removed the vial from his coat. The pure, gleaming blue of the fluid inside was unmistakable.

"A whole *vial* of the Father's life? How did you get ...?" She held the lamp close to the vial. "Wait—is this what you put on my lips before?" She put her fingers to her mouth, as if touching a sacred object.

Adam poured the precious liquid into his hand and rubbed it on his arms. "Stand back."

She retreated several paces.

His skin glistened blue in the lamplight. As he unsheathed the sword, the hue changed from blue to purple. With one hand, he lifted the great weapon above his head, paused, then slashed downward and across, impacting the boulder.

The blow cracked like a clap of thunder, and the stone shattered. Bits of debris pelted Abigail's whole body. Her ears rang, and grains of dirt crunched in her teeth as sunlight lit the dust-filled cave.

"Adam, that was ... I've felt power from the wind before, but it was never more than a mist. That was ..." She looked again at the vial. "How did you get that much?"

"The wind isn't the only one who gives life. I'll show you how to get much more—enough to wield the sword. But right now we need to go. Stay close to me, and *don't look at the fruit*."

She took his hand, and they stepped out of the cave. It was several minutes before her cramping fingers made her realize her nails had been digging into Adam's skin. Everything was on the line. If she couldn't escape with Adam's help, she would never escape. It was now or never, and success now seemed … unlikely.

Adam turned his head and the glint of the sun revealed something Abigail hadn't noticed in the darkness of the cave. She regarded him with a curious tip of her head. "Glasses?"

He took them off and held them up toward the sun. "They're hard to see, aren't they. So thin. The Ruler gave them to me. Oh, and he gave me this too." He returned the spectacles to his face and pulled a leather-bound booklet from his pack.

She wrinkled her nose. "Eww. It stinks."

"Tell me about it. But this little book is important. We'll need it for our escape."

Abigail took the volume in two fingers, holding it at arm's length, and read the title. "Stay Alert?"

"The Ruler wrote that on the cover when he gave it to me."

"If it came from the Ruler, why does it smell like"—Abigail's mind went blank. They had entered a dense section of the orchard and were surrounded by peach trees. Temptation came, not as an alluring siren, but as a springing trap, unheeded until it's too late.

Abigail could see nothing but the countless balls of enticement hanging from branches all around her. She tried to remember what she had been saying, but couldn't.

I need to think about the happiness room.

But her mind refused to let go of its fixation on the fruit. It was as though the peaches were shouting at her, preventing any other thought from entering her mind. The last time she had enjoyed a peach played like a vivid drama in her imagination. Her mouth watered. Every cell in her body demanded a taste.

Her hand rose as if with a mind of its own, plucked a peach, and brought it to her mouth. Her whole body tensed in anticipation.

Just as she began to bite down, the peach fell to the ground. A strong hand had clamped her wrist.

“No, Abigail! Please!”

She stumbled, but the hand on her wrist held her up. It was pulling her. She wanted that peach, but she also wanted to be pulled away. She leaned on Adam as they returned to the cave.

Back inside, her delirium lifted and she understood what had just happened.

She steadied herself against the wall. “I told you this would happen,” she said through tears. “I can’t do it. I’ll never be able to do it. Just leave me here.”

Adam had done what he could, and she loved him for it. But there comes a point where no one, no matter how earnest, can rescue a lost soul.

I’m just too far gone.

Adam released her wrist. Her knees gave way and she slid down against the wall to the cave floor.

The darkness of the cave seemed to have a gravitational pull. She stared into the blackness. If she gave in to the impulse to wander back into the caverns, would she be devoured quickly?

Then this whole nightmare would be over.

Chapter 11

Abigail averted her gaze, ashamed, as Adam knelt in front of her.

"I'm not leaving you," he said, "and you're not staying here. I'm going to get you to the clearing, and then we'll have help from the others to get you out of the orchard."

"I appreciate you pulling me away from the peaches, Adam. But it's a long way from here to the clearing. There's just no way. It doesn't matter how much I prepare myself. There is no 'off' button for my cravings."

"Actually, there is."

"There is what?"

"An 'off' button. The desires *can* be temporarily turned off."

He reached into his pack, but Abigail put her hand on his arm. "What are you going to do—give me another cottage piece? It's no use, Adam. As soon as I see the fruit, my mind goes blank. I forget everything I've ever learned."

"That's why you need this," he said as he drew a small cottage piece from the pack. He ran a string through it and placed it over her head.

Abigail inspected the wooden pendant. "It's a carving," she mused, running her finger over its contours. "*Such detail.* Who carved this? You can even see the tiny muscles straining in the child's arms."

"It's a father and daughter. The box at her feet is a gift she just opened."

"And she's squeezing her father in gratitude," Abigail said, still marveling at the statuette. "What a beautiful piece. Thank you."

Breaking from her fixation on the pendant, she looked again at Adam. "But how does this help me turn off my cravings?"

"I'll ask you the question Charles asked when he gave it to me. Why isn't the girl crying?"

"Crying? Why would she? She just received a precious gift."

"One gift. But how many gifts has she *not* received?'

"What do you mean? There are millions of things she didn't receive."

"Exactly. So how can she be so happy while being deprived of a million good gifts?"

Abigail nodded slowly. "Because … her attention isn't on any of the things she didn't receive—only on what she *did* receive."

Abigail studied the piece again. Something inside her melted at the touching display of happy thankfulness between daughter and father. It made her wish she was that little girl.

Adam took the piece from her fingers and turned it over. "There's an inscription on the bottom."

Squinting, she struggled to make out the miniscule print. "Si … Silence greed with … gratitude." She looked up at Adam. "What does that mean?"

"The problem in your heart is greed, right? Greed for fruit."

"I've never really thought of it that way, but … I guess so."

"There's a reason your desires for fruit aren't overpowering here in the cave, but out there you lose control. It's because seeing stimulates greed—like fuel on a fire."

"So what are you going to do—blindfold me?"

"No, we're going to turn off the greed. It's impossible to feel both greed and gratitude at the same time. That's why the girl was happy and not crying even though she was deprived of a million gifts."

"So you're saying if I feel gratitude like this girl, I'll be able to walk through the orchard without being overpowered with temptation?"

"If there's enough joy in your gratitude—yes. You won't even see the fruit."

She folded her arms. "Isn't that kind of a simplistic solution? Just say 'thank you' and overpowering cravings go away?"

"It would be simplistic if gratitude were merely saying 'thank you.' But that's not what gratitude is. Think about it. You can say those words without really being grateful, right?"

"Yeah. I suppose."

"So then, what is gratitude?"

She thought a long time. "Enjoying the gift?"

"That's closer, but isn't it also possible to enjoy a gift and still not be thankful—like a man who enjoys his wife's cooking and housework, but pays no attention to her?"

She thought for a moment and again acknowledged the point.

"Look again at the figurine."

She examined it, then spoke softly. "She's not just enjoying the gift. She's enjoying the love expressed in the gift."

Adam lifted her to her feet and led her outside the cave. "Hold up your hands."

She wrinkled her forehead.

"Just do it."

She lifted her right hand.

"Both of them."

"Okay. Is this a robbery, or what?"

"Look at your ten fingers. *That's* what will get you through to the clearing. I want you to go through the last ten times the Father has shown kindness to you, one at a time. Each time you think of one, take a moment to relive it. Chew on it like a choice steak. Extract all the joy you can—not from the gift, but from the Father's love expressed in the gift. Remember the little girl."

Adam took hold of her index finger. "When you've thoroughly enjoyed the first one, put this finger down and move to the next one. Don't stop until all ten fingers are down."

Abigail looked again at her fingers, then at Adam.

"Stay close," he said and led her out of the cave.

She knew Adam couldn't prevent her from taking a piece of fruit if she chose to, but having him with her helped. Each time he saw her glance at some fruit, he held up his ten fingers and wiggled them. She refocused on the Father's gestures of love, and gratitude returned.

But fruit was everywhere. Branches hung so low and close together that fruit continually brushed across her face. It littered the ground. Her skin grew sticky from juice as they made their way through the maze of temptation.

A melon on the ground caught her eye. She tried to look away but couldn't. It held her. She *wanted* it. Desire churned and roiled within her. Her heart pounded as she felt her will slipping from her control.

She took hold of the pendant and fixed her attention on the girl and the tightness of her hug. If she could be that girl, just for a moment—if she could feel that way ... Her mind raced, searching for a gift—a specific gesture of the Father's love.

A breeze arose, and she drew a deep breath. The cool, crisp air carried the sweet scent of some nearby lilacs and brought a flash of childhood memories. Playing with friends in the fields, picking flowers for her mother, enjoying the freedoms of childhood and the wonders of the created world, lying in the grass and finding shapes in the clouds. It's amazing, she thought, how a momentary scent can bring back such vivid memories—and not just the events, but the feelings that went with them.

She closed her eyes and inhaled again. Such a familiar fragrance. Why was this time special? Why hadn't these memories arisen all the other times she brushed by the flowers?

The breeze leafed through her curled bangs. Sweeping them from her eyes, she understood. The Father had sent the wind to enable her to enjoy one of his most common gifts—a breath of air. She touched the box in the carving. For her, the gift was a simple lung full of air—air that carried in it a moment's enjoyment of the delights of her childhood and the love of her Father. She took thousands of breaths every day, but this one—this breath the Father had enabled her to enjoy.

That breath was more than a gift. It was a gesture of the Father's love. It was his gentle kiss on her cheek. She wanted to respond. Grateful love for the Father swelled inside her.

She held up the figurine. *The girl. It's … me.*

Another melon lay in the center of the path before her. She nudged it out of the way with her foot. It rolled up against a log and came to a stop. The rind convulsed, then split open, releasing an army of black, frenzied insects that scurried into the surrounding shrubs.

Ew! I was about to eat that? She realized the moment of insight and clarity was yet another gift, and her heart swelled with love for the Father.

Finally, the dense orchard gave way to a spacious meadow. Abigail looked up, startled, and scanned the meadow. Then she faced the section of the orchard they had just exited.

"It worked!" She grabbed Adam by both shoulders, as if to press her exuberance into his bones. "I thought it would be impossible, but …"

She held up the carving and turned it, marveling. Then she squeezed it in her palm. "I've resisted fruit before, but it always felt like a loss—like I was missing out. But this …" she opened her arms wide and spun in a circle. "I feel like I've gained the world."

Adam laughed. "Yeah, gratitude can do that." He took her hands and joined her in another twirl.

"It's a great victory. And this meadow is a nice respite. But we're still surrounded by the vineyard. We need to join up with the others and then get out of the vineyard altogether. He pointed to the hills on the far side of the field. "We're almost there. The clearing I told you about is just over those hills. Hopefully the others will be there."

He opened his pack, releasing a sickening stench. "You dropped this," he said as he pulled out the book he had shown her in the cave. "But it's important. It's the prince's strategy manual." He held it open. "These are all his tactics."

She accepted the booklet. "How did you get the prince's manual?"

"A guardian seized it from one of the regional powers near the city and gave it to Charles. He told me to bring it to you."

She turned to the first page. Tracing with her finger, she scanned the paragraphs. "So, we'll know exactly what the enemy will do?"

"That's right. The Ruler assured me that the prince never deviates. All we have to do is learn his strategies and stay alert."

*****

With a grunt, Layth heaved a dead tree he had dragged up from the valley onto the woodpile.

Kailyn raised her eyebrows. "Planning on a bonfire?"

"It'll get cold tonight. Don't want to be huntin' for firewood in the dark."

"We will need every bit of it," Charles said. "This is dangerous territory. We'll have to stand guard in shifts through the night. Where's Watson?"

"I am here." Watson emerged from the trees carrying a stump.

He threw it on the pile and it rolled right back off, scraping his ankle. He kicked at the offending lumber but missed. The errant swipe landed his foot in a low tree branch, where it wedged, causing Watson to lose his balance and fall. He landed on his back, bare foot upraised, shoe and sock still in the tree.

Layth extended a hand. "You okay?"

Watson allowed the big man to pull him back to his feet. He rubbed his back and turned his leg to get a look at the scrape. "I will live."

"Not talking about your ankle." Layth sat on a log and motioned for Watson to join him. "You lost your sister."

Watson retrieved his footwear from the tree and sat next to Layth. He slipped the sock gingerly over his cut, then fastened his shoe.

Charles joined them on the log. "I can't imagine your anguish. But remember, the Ruler never takes more than he gives."

Watson's bowed head remained low. "I know. But …" He lifted his face. "The Ruler knows everything. Why would he send us on a mission he knew was doomed to fail?"

"*Did* it fail?" Charles asked. "What does the Ruler require of us?"

"To do as he commands."

Charles shook his head. "That's secondary. His requirement is that we love what the Father loves. Actions follow affections."

Charles stood and placed the stump on the woodpile. "So, did you come here because you loved the Ruler—and Abigail?"

Watson nodded.

"Did you desire her restoration and joy?"

"More than anything."

"Did you come because you love the orchard or the city's gold?"

Watson's faced reddened. "I hate them both."

"Well then," he raised his arms in victory, "mission accomplished! You did what the Ruler requires. The outcome is in his hands."

"I suppose. But I can't help feeling this whole effort has been a waste—everything we went through in the gorge, the battles, the—"

"You *feel* like it's a waste? So what? Which is more reliable—the Ruler's word or your feelings? If he says something is worthwhile, then—"

Watson's eyes widened. "I can't believe it."

"You *must* believe—"

"No, not that. Look!" Watson jumped to his feet and pointed. His normal, composed manner gave way to a child's excitement. The others scurried to his side. "Down there in the meadow. See?"

"That's her!" Kailyn said. "It's Abigail!"

"And is that Adam with her?" Watson asked.

"Sure is," Layth said. "Arrived this morning. Guess I forgot to mention I ran into him during the quake." Layth looked at their shocked expressions and shrugged. "With the hubbub and all."

Watson waved his arms. "Abby! Abbyyyy!" The whole group shouted, with Layth's thunderous voice booming above them all.

"It is no use," Watson said. "They are making too much noise tramping through that dry grass. We'll have to get closer."

Charles grabbed Watson's arm. "Hold on. A meadow like that can be dangerous. It's prime hunting ground for predators. The tall grass gives them cover."

The group scanned the meadow. "There," Kailyn said, pointing. "At the north end. Do you see that?"

Watson squinted. "I cannot tell. I—"

"You're right," Charles said. "Something's there. It's moving."

Kailyn gripped Layth's arm. "They're walking straight toward it!"

Chapter 12

"Hold on," Abigail said. She used one hand to balance herself against Adam and the other to remove her shoe. She turned it over, and with a shake, liberated three large pebbles. She repeated the action on the other foot, muttering. "These shoes are worthless. They have holes in the sides."

Adam held out his hand. "Let me see."

His movement disrupted her balance, and she hopped twice on one foot before steadying herself with her unclad foot in the dirt.

"Why did you do that? Now my sock is all dirty."

"Sorry. I didn't mean—"

"Just give me the shoe." She snatched it from his hand and with a couple more hops, shoved it on.

They resumed walking, and it wasn't long before another of earth's little irritants made its way into her footwear.

She started to bend down again, and her satchel swung down in front of her face. She grimaced and turned her face away. "Ugh!" She jerked the bag open, took hold of the *Stay Alert* booklet, and crammed it farther down into the bag. "Isn't there something we can do about the smell of that book? It's giving me a headache."

Adam stopped and faced her. "Want to tell me what's going on?"

"What do you mean? The book smells, and my shoes are …"

Adam folded his arms.

Abigail picked at a clasp on her bag. Then she sighed. "I don't know. I'm just … not in a great mood. I don't know why. Maybe it's hormones. Can we just …" she nodded forward and they resumed walking.

Before long, she noticed a blackberry plant to the side of the path. She dropped a step or two behind Adam. After he passed it, she glanced to the sides and behind, then quickly stooped and picked a berry.

Probably shouldn't have done that. But it won't be a problem. I'm not going to eat it. I don't even feel tempted.

She rolled the little bundle of juice between her fingers as she walked. *Everyone around here eats all the fruit they want. Berries and grapes are my only vice, mostly. The Ruler will understand. I just walked through that whole grove without caving. I've done so well. I deserve one guilty pleasure—especially after all I've been through.*

A breeze wafted through the field and her bangs fell in front of her eyes. *Who am I kidding? Fruit is fruit. Disobedience is always wrong.*

She rolled the blackberry again. *Why does this have to be so hard?* She swatted at the tuft of hair in her eyes and missed, scratching her face. *Argh! I don't think anyone understands what it's like for me.*

The breeze gusted again. Those words—the ones that had just run through her mind—they were … She tucked the blackberry in a pocket and fished the *Stay Alert* book from her pack. She flipped to where she had left off. Yes, there it was—all of it.

First, the irritability of a hungry soul deprived of real food. Then rationalization for getting close to the fruit. Then thinking it is "probably" wrong, leaving a door open with the word "probably." Then an arrogant confidence that "I can handle it," combined with self-pity.

She turned the page. The next heading was "Curiosity." The paragraph began, "Whisper to the subject, 'I wonder if this is a sweet one. I could take just a tiny, little taste. That wouldn't count as *eating* fruit.'"

She read on. "Then after the taste, 'Well, I've already blown it now. I might as well just finish off the whole bunch and try to do better tomorrow.'"

She closed the book. *I've fallen for these strategies so many times. I shouldn't need a book to warn me of it.*

She stopped short. "Adam, did you see that?"

"What?"

Backing up a few steps, she pointed. "I think it's right up there, straight ahead."

Adam joined her retreat as he squinted to see.

They both jumped when a flock of quail sprayed up from the grass fifty yards ahead. The same moment, a huge lion sprang from his hiding place.

Abigail hurled the berry as far as she could heave it and reached for Adam's sword.

"No," he said. "Fight when you have to. Run when you can."

They spun, breaking for the south end of the meadow where they had entered.

Abigail knew her deformities would slow her, but she didn't think it would be this bad. For Adam, the pace was little more than a brisk walk. But she was thankful he still stayed between her and the charging beast.

A glance over her shoulder sent chills down her spine. The lion was closing fast.

Looking forward, Abigail slid to a stop. Alexander stood directly before them, holding a thick, iron bar.

*****

"Don't stop!" Adam shouted. He pointed to the west. "That way."

She turned sharply to her right. Alexander started toward her, but Adam intercepted him.

"Out of my way!" Alexander demanded.

Adam pulled his leather belt from his pack and tied it around his waist. He ran his fingers over the familiar engraved lettering, *Mirror Room ... Blood Room ... Promise Room ... Room of Delights ...* The belt stiffened, then all his clothes became as impenetrable as armor, complete with a helmet.

As Adam squared off with the little soul, the lion lunged, clamping his jaws on Adam's shoulder. The impact knocked Adam to the ground, but the lion yelped and ran off. *What in the world? Did he crack a tooth—or ...*

Alexander sneered. "You think the Father will be satisfied with this lame rescue effort? You've failed!" As Adam regained his feet, Alexander charged, ramming his shoulder into Adam's chest.

With feet made nimble by the belt, Adam cut to the side and watched Alexander's flailing body glance off his chest and tumble into the dirt. "My Father is pleased with me, not because of how well I perform, but because of what he did in the blood room."

Alexander recovered quickly and came at Adam with his bar. He swung the weapon with both hands, smashing it against the side of Adam's helmet. "It's because of you that Abigail was captured to begin with. Nothing you could ever do will make up for the damage you've done."

The blow brought Adam to one knee but only stunned him. He stood. "I don't have to make up for anything. The damage I've done has been forgiven—all of it, forever."

Alexander stared wide-eyed at the bend Adam's helmet had just put in his iron weapon.

Adam drew his sword and pressed it to Alexander's throat. "You elevate your knowledge of this world above the word of the one who made it. You use the wind of your own mouth to deny the existence of wind. And you speak of the laws of cause and effect while claiming all existence had no cause."

Alexander scoffed. "Even if I don't know the first cause, that doesn't make the myths of the cottage true. Don't you see, Adam? Those teachings were made up by people who talked themselves into believing in a world they want to be true, and you accept it on blind faith."

"I accept it because of incontrovertible proof. The creation, prophecy, the Ruler recovering from death blows in the blood room. Given the evidence, it is your doubt, not my faith, that is irrational."

Alexander pushed the sword away, rolled, and came to his feet.

Adam lunged. "You accuse us of forcing reality to fit what we want to believe, but who does that more than you?"

"What are you talking about?"

"Your beliefs on morality, for one. You believe right and wrong are defined by whatever feels right or wrong to you. How convenient! Of all the countless people in the world with differing ideas of morality, you are the only ones who happened to be born with feelings about right and wrong that match reality perfectly? And right and wrong just so happen to fit hand in glove with whatever you like or don't like. That sounds to me like the definition of someone who believes what he wants to believe."

Flat on his back, Alexander flailed to shield himself from the unrelenting blows of Adam's sword.

"You're betting your eternal existence on the gamble that there is no final justice—no Creator you will have to answer to, no Judgment Day. You're so sure there won't be eternal consequence for any of the evil things you've done. How fortunate for you! Tell me, what empirical test did you run to prove all this? What observation did you make of this world to verify the nonexistence of things beyond this world?"

Alexander countered only with a hateful scowl.

"Since you won't speak, I'll tell you the answer. You believe all this nonsense because you imagine it gives you freedom—freedom to live the way you want, freedom from the laws of the Ruler. But can't you see? You're not free. You're enslaved to your own stomach. You submit to the tyranny of the god of your appetites. Every morning you bow to the trough. And for what? Moments of pleasure followed by emptiness, regret, and a pointless life."

Adam stood over his defeated foe, heartbroken, wishing Alexander would come to his senses. *Perhaps he will one day.* He placed some cottage pieces in Alexander's limp hand. *I hate this fighting. But Abigail should be safe by now.*

*****

A quarter-mile west of the meadow, Abigail cowered. Her back against a cliff, the lion blocked her only way of escape. Saliva dripped from his mighty jaws as he closed on her.

If only I had taken the sword! She scanned the ground for a stone, a branch, anything.

The monstrous creature seemed to be grinning as he crept closer.

She forgot to breathe. Even her shaking stopped as paralysis overtook her. She squeezed her eyes shut and awaited her fate.

Chapter 13

Even with her eyes closed, Abigail could feel the lion looming, the heat of his breath sending a ripple of dread through her body. The creature erupted with a thunderous roar that yanked all breath from her lungs and drove her to her knees.

Then another angry roar, and she opened her eyes. The lion lurched to its left and retreated into the woods dragging a javelin lodged in its side.

"Abigail!" She had never been happier to hear Layth's voice. Just behind him stood Watson, Kailyn, and Charles. Moments later, Adam arrived. The depth of joy in their happy reunion was so foreign to this empty land that the fruit trees themselves seemed to recoil.

"We saw you in the meadow," Charles said. "We were on the ridge above you, but we couldn't get to you in time to warn you about the lion."

Watson wrapped Abigail in a tight hug, his arms trembling. "We thought you were dead," he whispered.

"Alexander must not have known about the caverns under the south end of the orchard," Adam explained. "He thought he had buried her alive."

Watson let go of his sister and grabbed Adam's hand with both of his, then gave him a heartfelt hug.

Layth put a hand on Adam's shoulder. "From up here, it looked like she spotted the lion before you did buddy. You need to stay alert or you'll be lion lunch."

"It was because of this," said Abigail, taking the book from her belt. "It's the prince's strategy book. It showed me exactly where to look."

"We'll need that," Charles said. "It will take that and every weapon we have to make it out of the orchard." He pointed to the sword on Adam's hip. "Especially that one."

Adam unsheathed it and mimicked the strike that felled Alexander. "It already saved me once today." His powerful arms still glowed purple.

"Show them the vial," Abigail said.

When he removed it from his coat, she took it and held it up to Watson. "Have you ever seen anything like this?"

Watson reached into his own pocket and produced an even larger vial, filled to the top with the empowering blue fluid.

"I've only seen mists of this before. How is this even possible?"

"I had a … setback on the way here," Watson began. "A battle with temptation to which I, regrettably, succumbed. I thought I had lost, having consumed several berries. I learned, however, that the battle was not lost when I failed. Rather, the battlefield merely changed. It went from a struggle over whether I would eat fruit to a struggle over whether I would delay returning to the Father to confess and restore closeness with him. The moment I chose to return, the Ruler appeared, and he taught us how to receive more of this"—he held up the vial—"than we had ever imagined possible."

"It comes from closeness with the Ruler," Kailyn said, displaying her own vial. "Every time your heart draws near to him to enjoy his colors, he adds to the vial."

"May I?" Abigail asked, still holding Adam's vial.

"Take as much as you want."

She rubbed the fluid on both arms, handed the vial back, and pointed to the sword.

He extended it, handle first, and she gripped it with both hands. When Adam let go, the weighty weapon slipped from her grasp and fell to the dirt. The group stood in silence.

Layth stepped forward, took up the blade with one hand, and returned it to Adam. Then he faced Abigail. "When's the last time you had a decent meal?"

He turned to Charles. "No one can fight when they're starving. Let's eat. We can worry about the sword later."

"Couldn't agree more," Charles said with a wink.

Layth and Watson encircled the fire pit with logs for seating, and within the hour, Adam and Charles had the meal ready.

Stories, laughter, and words of encouragement crisscrossed the circle as the ravenous squad of rescuers enjoyed their first full meal together since Charles arrived in the lowlands. Abigail closed her eyes and took in the sounds of family love. Everyone seemed to be so thoroughly enjoying the meal.

She looked down at her plate. *I should eat,* she thought as she appraised the entree. *Why does this feel like such a chore?*

With a push of resolve, she lifted a fried chicken leg to her mouth, nibbled, then set it down again, exhausted from the effort.

Layth stared at her for a moment, then motioned to her plate with his cup. "That grub ain't gonna eat itself."

"Do you taste anything?" Adam asked.

"A little." She turned her gaze away from the circle. A barn swallow flitted from tree to tree. She mused over the wonder of the creation, and the gentle care the Father took in providing for every creature every day.

The swallow swooped down, plucked a worm from the ground, and carried it back to its nest. Abigail left the circle and inched as close as she could to the nest without scaring the bird. Several chicks, just hatched, stretched their necks, beaks wide open, desperate for a morsel.

A gentle breezed brushed Abigail's face and whispered. *Look at those chicks. If your heart were like that toward the Ruler, you would have your smile back. The portion size is limited only by the stretch of your jaws.*

"Time for dessert," Adam called.

Abigail made her way back to the group and took a seat next to Watson, who put his arm around her and pulled her close.

Adam stood in the middle of the circle and began unfolding a tiny cottage piece that simply said, "Good sorrow/bad sorrow."

"Good sorrow," he explained, "drives you to the Father. Bad sorrow makes you give up. If you listen to your feelings, you will destroy yourself. When you stumble, instead of listening to yourself, *talk to yourself.* But don't talk to yourself about your failure. Talk to the Father about your failure and talk to yourself about the Father."

"Preach to your soul. Remind yourself constantly what he's like toward those who turn back to him—merciful, patient, gracious, tender, slow to anger, and overflowing in love. His anger remains for a night but rejoicing comes in the morning. He restores what is broken, redeems the prisoners, and revives the dead."

When he finished speaking, he sat beside Abigail and Watson.

"That was delicious," Abigail said. "Thank you."

Adam smiled and reached for his cup.

Abigail lifted her arm and placed it next to Adam's, contrasting the blue on her skin with his purple.

"Good eye," said Charles. "The color changes when the fluid is activated."

"How is it activated?" she asked. "Is there some kind of catalyst?"

Charles smiled. "The catalyst is the one thing that draws you nearer to the Ruler than anything else—*trust*. You are never closer to him than when you're trusting him. And when you trust, his blood activates the fluid. That's when the real power comes."

Charles stood and began collecting the empty plates. "We'll talk more about it tomorrow. I suggest you don't stay up too late. We'll want to get an early start."

The first gleam of dawn found the camp clear and the six friends already making their way westward. Layth led the way with Charles guarding the rear. Watson and Adam walked on either side of Abigail, who carried the sword.

Abigail stumbled and Adam caught her.

"You look tired," he said.

She rubbed her eyes. "I didn't sleep much. I had a nightmare that woke me up and I couldn't go back to sleep. I just kept thinking about it all night."

"What was it about?"

"A rattlesnake dropped on me in a dark cave. I screamed and threw it away as hard as I could. Then a guardian appeared and said—"

Adam finished her sentence. "'Remember the vigor with which you cast it.' I had the same dream. It's to prepare you for the battle. When it comes time to use the sword, remember that dream. Remember how you felt. Unless you hate the enemy like you hated that snake, you will fall."

Abigail walked in silence, trying to imagine what the battle would be like. Who would she face? Would she hesitate in the decisive moment? And, if so, would she remain locked in the orchard forever?

"Your skin," Adam said, touching Abigail's forearm.

She lifted her arm. A slight purple glow tinted her skin. A smile warmed her face. *It's happening!* She touched the sword. "Maybe I *will* be ready to strike when the moment comes."

Chapter 14

Mid-morning, they stopped for rest. When Charles took a seat next to Abigail, she knew what was on his mind. "So far, so good," she assured him. "No temptations."

"*No* temptations? How could that be? There's an apple tree right over there." He swept his arm in a wide arc. "You've had fruit around you all morning. How is it possible that you haven't been tempted?"

"I don't know. I guess it's because I'm here with all of you. I'm not going to eat fruit right in front of everybody."

"Do you know why that is?"

She smirked. "I have a feeling I'm about to."

"It's because we assist your fear."

"You mean, you help me not be afraid?"

"No. We help you *be* afraid."

"What?" She looked at him, then shot a glance at Watson, who only shrugged.

Charles explained. "The more you love someone, the more you fear that person's displeasure. If a stranger doesn't like you, you hardly care. But if your mother or father or a dear friend disapproves, it matters a great deal. The more you prize intimacy, the more frightening the thought of losing that intimacy."

"Makes sense," she said.

"You understand that life flows freely to us from the Ruler when we love him. But you can't love him without fearing him."

"I do fear him. I fear his displeasure."

"Do you? In the meadow, just before you spotted the lion, you picked something up. Was it fruit?"

She hung her head.

"Just before you picked it up, I saw you look to your left and right and behind."

"You saw that?"

He laid a hand on her shoulder. "I'm not trying to shame you, Abigail. I also saw you throw it away, which is commendable. I only bring it up to ask, why did you look left and right before picking it up?"

"I … I just … you know, I wanted to make sure no one would see me."

"Because if someone whose opinion mattered was watching, then they might not approve?"

"Yes."

"Then why did you look left and right, but not *up*, toward your Creator? You wouldn't have taken it had there been disapproving eyes to your left or right. But what of the eyes above?"

Her stomach knotted. The truth was, her Creator had been the farthest thing from her mind in the moment of temptation. The realization stunned her.

A squeeze from Charles' hand recaptured her attention. "I know you love the Ruler. Of course it would matter to you if he were standing right beside you in times of temptation. The problem is one of awareness. We all forget to look up because the Father is invisible. So is the wind. And the Ruler isn't always standing nearby. But"—he gestured to the rest of the group—"you *can* see us."

She looked around and regarded each face.

Charles went on. "Being with others who love the Ruler assists you in fearing the Ruler's displeasure. Our presence stands in for his presence. That's why you haven't been tempted all morning."

"It's true," Watson said. "It was when Kailyn and I became separated briefly that I fell to temptation. And it was not until Kailyn and Layth were with me that I felt the shame I would have felt had the Ruler been present."

"We'll all stay together to get you home," Charles said. "But we won't always be with you. You can't avoid being alone sometimes. So you must learn to live your life in a glass house—as exposed and open as you can make it. That's what the Ruler means by 'walking in the light.' Privacy is comfortable, but deadly."

"Lone rangers are dead rangers," Layth added.

The group came together and made a pact—if any one of them ate a piece of fruit, they would confess it to someone else in the group the same day.

As each one pledged commitment to the pact, the lowland cloud broke, shadows retreated, and the friends walked in the light the rest of the way to the western exit from the orchard.

As the border came into view, Abigail halted.

"What's wrong?" Adam asked as the rest of the friends gathered around her. "Why did you stop?"

*****

Gibbor and the other eleven guardians stood ready. Seventy warriors swarmed the area, surrounding the friends. The prince, Adramelech, and his lieutenants blocked the exit—weapons drawn.

Gibbor eyed the evil horde and pondered his next move. The humans carried on, oblivious to the battle about to erupt around them—although Charles looked like he might sense something. *Hopefully*, Gibbor thought.

Even if the guardians could somehow hold their own against the warriors, not even Gibbor could match the prince.

*****

"Come on, Abigail," Kailyn urged. "You're so close. You're almost free. Just a little farther and we'll be out."

"And then what? Go to the banquet hall and face the Ruler? Look at me. How could I stand before him like this?"

Kailyn took Abigail's face in her hands. "Abigail, *he loves you.* He wants you back—that's why he sent us. Why do you think the Ruler suffered for you? It wasn't because of how beautiful or valuable you were. He did it because of how beautiful and valuable he wants to make you. After the price he paid for you, do you think he's going to cast you aside now?"

"That's easy for you to say. You haven't done what I've done. You've never walked away for this long."

"Are you saying the Ruler's sacrifice was enough to cover my evil but not yours?" Kailyn asked. "Don't you remember the blood room? What the Ruler did in that room will apply to you if you trust him. What matters is what's in your heart, not what's in your past."

"Abby," Watson added, "your heart is condemning you, not the Ruler. Which assessment matters—yours, or his?"

"I know what you're saying is true, but every time I picture myself standing before him in all his purity and perfect holiness, I can't imagine feeling anything other than unbearable shame."

*****

Three burning arrows from the prince had lodged deep into Abigail's heart. Charis, Abigail's guardian, leaned in to Gibbor. "The traces of faith remaining in her are going up in smoke. I can't get through to her."

"Look," said Sol, pointing to Watson. "He took two arrows to the chest as well. Every time he sees his sister's deformities and remembers her former beauty and joy, he questions the Ruler's goodness and power. He keeps mumbling, 'How could he let this happen?'"

"I'm getting that with Kailyn too," said K-lion. "It's as if her shield were suddenly too heavy for her to lift."

Gibbor grimaced as each of the humans lowered their shields. Then he looked to the west. *Where is Levite?*

The warriors began to close. "What can we do against so many?" K-lion asked.

Gibbor straightened and drew a breath through his nose. "We can fight valiantly—and pray for wind."

"Is Levite coming?" asked Sol.

"If he doesn't …" Gibbor turned his attention to the prince. "Like I said—pray for wind."

On the prince's signal, several warriors moved in on the friends. The guardians blocked their way, meeting them nose to nose.

With deafening shrieks, the warriors attacked. The war was on.

Chapter 15

Abigail held her favorite cottage piece and ran her fingers over the inscription. “Ask, and you will receive if you believe and don’t doubt. The double-minded receive nothing. Persevere!”

The colors of this piece had so often dazzled her. The words had motivated her—fortified her. But in this moment, they were nothing but etchings on a splintered block of wood. She strained her eyes. Not a hint of color.

I’ve gone blind.

The piece dropped from her hand and disappeared in the grass. None of the inscriptions she remembered from the cottage seemed real anymore.

*****

Gibbor joined Charis in defending Abigail. But the other friends were also being overrun. Less than an hour into the battle, the cottage pieces Kailyn held in each hand both fell to the earth. Adam, Watson,

Layth—even Charles faltered. One piece after another tumbled from their grasp.

With the humans disarmed, the guardians' task went from difficult to impossible.

K-lion cried out from beneath a pile of frenzied warriors. Gibbor flew to him, sword a blur, and scattered the warriors like leaves in a tornado.

But this attracted the prince's attention. Just as K-lion regained his feet, the prince struck both guardians to the ground. With lightning-fast defensive maneuvers, Gibbor lured the prince away, but then more warriors fell upon K-lion.

"Fall back!" Gibbor ordered as he rocketed westward with the prince in pursuit.

*****

Three other guardians flew straight upward, then stopped above the clearing and drew their swords.

Adramelech pointed overhead and gave the order. "Brace!" He cursed himself for giving up such an advantage. He had expected the three to retreat, not to claim a strategic attack position from above. Now every warrior, including himself, was vulnerable.

The warriors arrayed in a practiced, defensive stance. Half gathered in a tight cluster with swords and lances raised upward. The rest formed a perimeter around the cluster to keep the guardians on the ground at bay.

But rather than attacking, the guardians on the ground disappeared into the trees.

Adramelech shivered as he imagined having to explain to the prince how he managed to allow all but three of the guardians to get away.

He turned his attention upward again. Without their comrades, there would be no escape for those three, higher position or not. They had sacrificed themselves for the others, and now he would make them pay.

As he prepared to give the attack order, the three guardians gave their own war cry. Adramelech resisted the impulse to cover his ears at the thunderous shout.

Now all the warriors turned their attention upward, startled that just three guardians could produce such a deafening roar.

Adramelech's attack order lodged in his throat as he reassessed the situation. Would three lone guardians commit suicide by diving into a horde of warriors?

In a symphony of cracking branches, the guardians in the trees exploded on the clearing from all sides.

But rather than a direct attack, they shot through the clearing in a crisscross pattern, sending the confused warriors stumbling backward into one another, flummoxed by the unconventional attack.

But no guardian laid a hand on any warrior. By the time Adramelech realized it wasn't an attack but a distraction, all the guardians had once again disappeared into the trees.

His eyes darted upward toward the three. *Gone!* Adramelech slammed his sword to the ground.

When the prince returned, Adramelech was glad to see his effort to capture Gibbor had failed. Perhaps the prince would be less eager to punish Adramelech for his own failure.

"The guardians escaped," he admitted. "But they won't get far. I sent three search teams. If they retreat to the west—"

"They won't," said the prince. "These guardians will never leave their charges." He peered into the trees. "They're close. Call the search teams back. Have them secure this clearing." He turned his glare to the humans. "I don't care about the guardians. Our objective is the humans, and we have them now. All we have to do is hold them."

The two spirits approached the doubting, defeated humans. "Do you see, Adramelech? Your shallow approach—merely tempting them to evil—was reversed in a moment when Kailyn repented. But what I'm doing here—destroying their faith—that will keep them from repentance so the damage will be permanent. As I said before—this kind falls only through unbelief."

Adramelech picked up a discarded shield and looked it over with a sneer. "It's amazing how weak they are without these," he said as he tossed it aside.

The prince nodded. "People will not risk losing everything for something they aren't sure is true."

The prince surveyed the battlefield and basked in the glory of his masterful victory. Not only had he held

Abigail, but he had captured five of the Ruler's most powerful agents—including one of the chief servers.

Approaching footsteps sounded from a dense grove of poplars to the west. Before the prince could turn to see, blinding pain brought him to his knees. Then another blow sent him skidding across the landscape. He tumbled, then slammed into a large peach tree, knocking it down.

The warriors drew back. Squinting into the blinding light, some began murmuring.

"It can't be!"

"How can this …?"

Levite stepped forward, sword drawn, fire in his eyes. The warriors backed away from the legendary guardian in a wide radius.

Gibbor and the other guardians emerged from hiding and returned to their charges.

Beside himself with rage, the prince regained his feet. He lifted his sword, ready to bring a world of pain on whatever misguided guardian had presumed to attack him from behind.

As his eyes adjusted to Levite's light, he saw beyond the massive guardian to the one who had struck him—a human. The prince nearly dropped his weapon. He shuddered and took a step back.

"Levi?" He hissed. *How could he be here?* He recalled his shock, centuries ago, when he received a similar blow from a boy with a sling. The same terrifying stench of faith that filled the valley of Elah that fateful day now pervaded this clearing.

*****

Abigail pointed to a dense grove of poplars to the west. “Listen. It sounds like someone’s coming.”

The group scanned the grove until the lone traveler emerged.

“Levi!” Kailyn ran and threw her arms around him.

Abigail was moved by Kailyn’s expression of pure, sisterly affection toward Levi, a man she hardly knew. It reminded her of what first drew Adam—the promise of family. The family love she had walked away from. A hole opened in her stomach as another layer of guilt descended on her.

After exchanging hugs and stories with the rest of the group, Levi explained why he had come. “My first assignment was to help you. The Ruler made it sound urgent, so I came as fast as I could. It doesn’t look like I’m needed here, from what I can see, but … whatever. The Ruler knows what he’s doing.”

When Levi uttered those words, words of simple trust in the Ruler’s plan, a loud crash echoed through the forest. Everyone turned in the direction of the sound.

“What was that?” Levi asked.

“Sounded like a tree falling,” Adam said. “Strange.”

Layth turned back to Levi and looked him up and down. “Did you bring a weapon?”

“Sort of, I guess. The wind gave me a gift when I went through the cottage and told me it was my weapon." Levi pushed his hands into his back pockets. "I really don't see how it would be useful in a fight though. I suppose I'll understand one day. For now, I'm just glad we're not in a war."

Watson and Layth exchanged knowing smiles.

Layth put a hand on Levi's shoulder. "Son, you'd be surprised at the warfare that's probably going on right now, here in this clearing, if you could see the spiritual world."

"More than *probably*," Kailyn said with a wary eye.

Levi scanned the quiet, lonely clearing and shrugged. "If you say so."

"So what's the gift?" Kailyn asked.

"Huh?"

"Your gift—from the wind. What is it?"

"Oh, right. I'm not sure what to call it, exactly. The Ruler handed me a little hand-carved chest. But when I opened it, it was empty."

"Did you notice any changes when you opened it?" Charles asked.

"Did I ever! When I lifted the top, everything changed. The walls, the floor, the doors—everything in the cottage became …" Levi searched for the word. "… solid. They had seemed real enough before, but when I opened the chest, I realized I had never even known what 'real' meant. Suddenly, the things that used to be hard to believe became … obvious. And trusting the Ruler came naturally."

"Shhh. I hear something." Kailyn pointed in the direction of the mysterious crash. "Someone's coming."

The king of the lowlands emerged from the trees, alone, smiling. "Ah, Abigail. I see you found your way out. Good for you."

Abigail wasn't sure if she was glad to see the king, or afraid—or both. His disarming smile broadened and Abigail was struck by his handsome face and his strong, yet gentle movements.

"I'm happy for you. I told you before I would never keep you in the orchard against your will. And now here you are."

Abigail gestured to the group. "These are my friends, Charles, Layth—"

"I know who they are." His eyes fixed on Charles. "I make it my business to know everything that happens in my kingdom."

He stepped past Abigail toward Charles. As he passed her, Abigail caught a whiff of the *Stay Alert* book in her satchel. Embarrassed, she pushed it down in the bag.

The king stepped oddly close to Charles. "So, you've come to bring Abigail back to the high country?"

Charles set his jaw.

"You needn't have," the king said. He turned again to Abigail. "If it is your desire to return to the high country, I wish you the best." With that, he stepped aside and motioned for her to pass.

*****

Gibbor and Charis stationed themselves between Abigail and the prince. Gibbor whispered to Charis. “Be alert. The prince is never more dangerous than when he takes human form like this. Don’t take your eyes off—”

The sickening sound of arrows plunging into a human heart made Gibbor spin. In an instant, he spotted Anzu concealed in the trees fifty yards behind Abigail.

Anzu tried to retreat, but Gibbor was upon him in an instant.

The evil warrior was ready. With surprising strength, he seized Gibbor by the throat.

Big Red left Layth and flew to help Gibbor. “No!” Gibbor croaked. “Mind the prince.”

Gibbor had fought many formidable warriors but rarely had he encountered one with such unrestrained rage—and deadly strength. Using his superior speed and skill, Gibbor twisted free and circled behind Anzu. He brought his sword down hard on Anzu’s back, but the massive warrior kept his feet. The gash seemed to only feed his strength as he turned and countered with a violent upward swing of his own.

Gibbor dodged, but the strike came so close that he felt the swoosh on his face and knew immediately that if Anzu ever connected, he would be finished.

Another slash. As Gibbor twisted, Anzu surprised him by dropping his weapon, rushing Gibbor, and slamming him to the ground.

From under Anzu, Gibbor glanced at Abigail just in time to see the prince, in his unseen form, draw his bow and set a razor-sharp arrow on the string. He lit the tip on fire and pointed it directly at Abigail's heart. The prince released, and the arrow flew.

Chapter 16

The king turned back to Abigail. "One more thing before you go. Just a word of caution, if I may. I don't mean to draw attention to your appearance. I mention it only because I know you love the Ruler and would never want to disappoint him—"

Abigail's chest and stomach tightened. Her friends' warmth and acceptance had made her forget her deformities. But the king's stark reminder renewed her despair, like waking from a good dream to a nightmarish reality.

The king continued. "You know how people in the banquet hall would stare if you showed up looking like that. I suggest before you go, you first—"

Charles' sword flashed with an explosion of brilliant colors. "First what? Clean herself up? How? Can a leopard scrub its spots?" He locked his gaze on the king. "Only the Ruler's blood can clean a soiled heart, and all this world's solutions do is *empty* the blood room of its power.'"

The king broke away from the stare-down with Charles and turned to Abigail. “If you want to go, go.” He started back the way he came, and as he brushed by Charles, he whispered. “You’ll regret this. You have no idea what’s coming.”

Charles whispered back. “I’m not the one who’s doomed.”

As the king walked off, Abigail stepped close to Charles. “What did you say to him?”

“The king of the lowlands is the prince of darkness in human form. He wanted to remind you of your past, so I simply reminded him of his future.”

Charles glared in the direction of the king’s retreat. “Don’t ever listen to him. The only way you can make yourself acceptable to the Ruler is by depending on the Ruler alone to make you acceptable. And he will. He made you beautiful before, and he’ll do it again. But if you try to make yourself pleasing, you will only make yourself detestable in his sight.”

He went on. “If you must look at your deformities, look at them as the Father looks at them—in the blood room, covered by the Ruler’s sacrifice. When the Father looks at one of his children, he sees the magnificent goodness of the Ruler credited to that child’s account. If you must look, look where the Father looks, and your eyes will meet his.”

His words came to her ears like food to a starving woman. A cottage saying she had memorized but hadn’t thought of in years came suddenly to mind, as if being spoken into her ear. “I found you in your ugliness, kicking in your blood. Then I touched you and made you the most beautiful of jewels."

Strength seeped into her soul. *The Ruler can fix me.*

*****

The prince's burning arrow, with its lethal tip, shattered on impact with Abigail's shield of faith and fell harmlessly to the ground.

The flash from Charles' sword and Abigail's shield distracted Anzu for the split-second Gibbor needed. In a single move, he twisted free and brought a thunderous blow down on Anzu's head. He left the dazed warrior on one knee and rejoined the other guardians.

Since Levi's arrival, all six friends had recovered their shields. Without Abigail's powerful weapon of joy, the friends were severely short-handed. But with the array of weapons the other friends held, they remained a formidable force.

Yes. Yes! Gibbor smiled as he watched the flurry of expert strikes from each of the friends' weapons.

When the prince tried to unnerve the group with worry or anxiety, Levi's unassailable child-like faith inspired them to trust the Ruler's promises.

Ten warriors surrounded Abigail and Kailyn with a cloud of darkness and tried to pull them down into depression. All ten got a taste of Layth's mighty javelin—his uncanny ability to find just the right cottage pieces to keep the friends' spirits up. That, combined with Watson's recounting of how the Ruler had so thoroughly forgiven him when he ate the berries, soon discouraged the ten warriors.

Abigail stopped to remove a pebble from her shoe. “These stupid shoes are—”

“Careful,” Watson warned. Given his analytical skills, the group had chosen him to carry the *Stay Alert* book. He pointed to the page he had been studying. “See this? An entire chapter on discontent and complaining. It is one of the prince’s most common attack angles.”

None of the prince’s strategies caught the group off guard. His every move met only impenetrable shields.

The presence of seven mountain people in the orchard had drawn a gathering of curious lowlanders. The more people gathered, the more attention they attracted until it became a large crowd. Murmuring within the crowd quickly escalated from whispering gossip to angry shouts.

“They’re mountain people!”

“What are you kids doing down here?”

“They’re here to cut down our trees!”

Gibbor assigned two guardians to assist Charis in guarding Abigail. “Surround her,” he said. “This angry crowd will trigger memories of the beating she endured at the earthquake. Do not let her give way to fear.”

Even as Gibbor spoke, Abigail turned toward the orchard and ran from the crowd.

"Go!" Gibbor ordered, and the three guardians followed her.

K-Lion nudged Kailyn, whispering. "See that mound? Not a bad platform."

Kailyn ascended the mound and lifted her voice above the din. "Yes, we are from the high country. And we invite you to join us there. It's so much better than anything in the orchard."

Abigail stopped. Was that Kailyn speaking to the crowd?

Yes, Charis whispered, pointing. *That's her up on that mound.*

"Your city is collapsing. Come with us before it's too late." The glow of Kailyn's double-edged dagger—strength and courage—shone on Abigail.

All five of the men were all occupied with other pockets of hostile lowlanders, yet not a trace of worry touched Kailyn's face. She planted her skinny legs like steel rods in the earth and stood her ground, speaking with the authority of the Ruler himself as if she owned these lowlands.

Charis whispered again to Abigail, *"You're no different than her. You belong to the Ruler. What can lowlanders do to you?*

Abigail looked around at the mob and spoke softly to herself. "They're like children on a playground." She threw her shoulders back and strode boldly westward, straight through the center of the crowd.

A woman spit on her and there were a few shoves, but she kept her attention on Kailyn whose courage infused Abigail with unnatural strength to keep moving. She wiped the spittle from her hair with her sleeve and stepped up on the mound at Kailyn's side.

"You will be honored for taking that abuse for the Ruler," Kailyn said. Then she pointed to the crowd. "And you who reject the Ruler will be punished."

"I've heard your Ruler is a man of love," shouted a man. He waved his arm across the crowd. "Would he condemn all these people for not following someone they have never seen?"

"They have never seen him because they refuse to look," said Watson, as he joined Kailyn and Abigail on the mound. "For a man of love, anger toward that which destroys the good is a moral necessity. One who loves, cares. And one who cares can never be apathetic about that which threatens the object of his love."

"Everyone who is not forgiven must answer for their rebellion," Kailyn added. She raised her hand to the crowd. "Every knee will bow before the Ruler of the kings of the earth, including yours. And your king's."

"I'm my own king," said another man.

Abigail ripped a peach from a tree and held it out toward the man. "*This* is your king. And it is a merciless tyrant. What does it give you other than regret? Why continue to serve it?"

The man stood silent, his face vacant. Then he approached the tree. He plucked a peach, examined it, and took a bite. He reached for another, and another, filling his arms.

The rest of the crowd surrounded the tree like a swarm of bees, devouring every peach and even gnawing on the branches.

"Leave them," K-lion whispered.

Kailyn sheathed her double-sided dagger, took Abigail's hand, and started back toward the others. When the friends had regrouped, they set out for the border.

Gibbor addressed the guardians. "Do all you can to guard your charges from discouragement. See that they do not grow weary in well-doing. None of them realize how far east the battle carried them. They have a long, difficult journey ahead."

*****

As the group walked, the lowland cloud thickened, and the friends frequently stumbled. After two hours of slogging uphill, climbing over downed trees, and straining to see in the cloud, Charles stopped. "This isn't right. It shouldn't be this dark."

"We need rest," Layth said. "That battle …" He wiped his brow. "It took a lot out of us."

"I don't think so, Layth. I'm tired too. But in this territory, the moment you get comfortable, you get captured. The warriors could attack at any time. And if they hit us now …" he scratched the back of his head, scanning the surrounding trees. "We don't want another fight right now."

He turned his gaze back to the group and was met with pleading faces.

"Okay. Ten minutes."

Twenty minutes later, only Charles remained awake. Sword drawn, he circled his slumbering friends, watching, listening. He would not allow a surprise attack.

He was pleased at how effective each of their weapons had been, but without Abigail's joy, they all lacked endurance. Even Charles' eyelids insisted on drooping.

He slapped his own face and shook himself. *I should wake them. We need to get moving.* He opened his mouth, but before he made a sound, a voice whispered. "No, don't disturb them. They're exhausted."

Charles froze in place, afraid to turn around.

The voice continued. "Even Layth wanted to stop. If you push ahead without his support, will they follow? Even if they do, they will resent you. They probably already question your leadership. Let them rest and you'll have their favor."

Charles recognized the voice—an old, intimate enemy. Still facing away, Charles' hand moved slowly to his sword.

"You're going to try to strike me down?" the voice said with a chuckle. "Why? You know I'm right. You remember the last time you tried to lead and no one followed, don't you? The humiliation. The sense of betrayal. The fear of losing your position of leadership. Do you want that again?"

Charles raised his sword and spun, setting the blade against the old man's throat. "What good is having their favor if I allow them to be captured? If I'm driven by fear of people's opinion of me, I am no longer the Ruler's servant."

With both hands, Charles pulled the sword back and swung with all his might. It sliced clean through the man's neck. His grey head fell to the ground, and his body crumpled.

Charles retrieved the head and held it up. He shuddered at the surreal experience—gazing into his own face as in a mirror. He tossed the head aside and dragged the headless, heartless body away from the group into a ravine.

He returned to his friends. "Wake up everyone! Time to go."

One-by-one, reluctant eyes opened. Amid a chorus of groans and yawns, Kailyn and Levi sat up. Then Watson. With a grunt, Layth rose and rubbed an ache out of his back. Adam sighed, put his hands on his knees, and pushed to his feet. Then he extended a hand and pulled Abigail up.

Charles lifted his arm. "Before we go, we need to do something about this cloud. Without light, we'll never make it."

His silent, penetrating gaze fell on each of the friends, moving from one to the next. Some returned only a puzzled look. Watson held Charles' gaze a moment, then gave a single shake of his head. Layth also met his gaze and whispered, "Not me."

When he came to Levi, the young man appeared mystified at first, then bowed his head. His lip quivered.

"Berries?" Charles asked.

Levi drew the remainder of an apple from his pocket and thrust it away. "I'm sorry," he whispered. "After the first bite, I knew it was a mistake. I was going to throw it away as soon as I got a chance. But I didn't want anyone to see."

Charles showed Levi the "Walk in the light" cottage piece and unfolded it for him. As he explained the meaning, he prepared to respond to Levi's objections. He knew from experience that most people resisted this cottage piece, especially those who were new to the high country and loved their privacy.

"Let me see that," Levi said, taking the piece. After a moment's examination, he said, "So this dark cloud we've been walking in—that was *my* fault?"

Before Charles could answer, a tear formed in Levi's eye. "I was wrong. Please forgive me. You have my word—I'll walk in the light from here on. No more hiding anything."

Levi lifted his eyes to Charles. "What's with the big smile? Are you laughing at me?"

"Not laughing. Rejoicing. You were wondering what good your weapon would be? There it is, right there. Most people don't have that kind of unquestioning acceptance when they're caught on the barbs of a cottage piece." Charles turned to the group. "That, friends, is what faith looks like."

A slap on the back from Layth sent Levi forward a step. "Well done, kid."

The cloud lifted.

*****

The prince addressed his warrior ranks: "Don't give up! I've faced the gift of faith before—and defeated it. It can be done, but not by slacking off whenever you get tired."

He burrowed his gaze into a warrior seated against a tree, nursing his wounds. "Get up! Fight, or I'll strike you down myself."

He turned to the other warriors. "What seems like an unwinnable war can turn if we keep attacking. Most humans give up quickly under pressure. And even the mightiest of men wear down eventually." He was shouting now. "I have won many battles against far more powerful enemies than these simply by outlasting their resistance. Do not relent!"

*****

The beleaguered humans pressed forward. With Levi's faith, Watson's discernment, Kailyn's courage, Charles' wisdom, Layth's encouragement, and Adam's insight, they held the warriors at bay. But without Abigail's joy, none of the weapons operated at full strength.

"This is a good fight," Charles said. "See it through. Your confidence will be richly rewarded if you don't throw it away. You need to persevere so that when you have done the Father's will, you will receive what he has promised. Stand firm!"

"I don't know if I can," Abigail said. "I'm not as strong as the others."

"You're stronger than you know. Strong enough to do everything the Father requires of you. We tend to give up far too soon." He paused and looked around.

"Do you see that log?" he said, pointing. He strode over to it, bent his knees, and heaved one end over his head.

"How long do you think you could hold this end up?" he asked.

Abigail shrugged.

"Here. Try it."

She maneuvered under the log.

"Got it?"

"Yeah, I think so."

Charles let go.

After twenty seconds, her arms began to shake. Ten more seconds, and she dropped the log to the side.

"Nice effort," Charles said. "Now imagine you have a baby who will be crushed if you let go. Then how long could you hold it? Longer than you ever thought possible. You would find hidden reserves. You would scream for help. You would hold, and hold, and hold."

Charles turned to the group. "Few people ever push their body to the limit—or even know where that limit is until there is an emergency. It's the same with the will. Resist long enough, the prince of darkness will flee."

Charles' face hardened and his voice took on a tone they all knew so well—that intonation that signaled he was about to say something of utmost importance.

"This is not a proverbial war. It's not a symbolic war. It's not a theoretical war. It's real—with real casualties. And the stakes are higher on both sides than in any war ever fought. When the Ruler says, 'resist the prince,' he means *resist*. Be fierce or be dead."

Charles went on. "Say, 'No!' to every evil thought within five seconds. Give it more unopposed time than that and it will lodge itself and become almost immovable. Say it out loud. Be warlike and fierce. Strike fast and strike hard or it is you who will be struck down."

*****

Abigail stood and cinched her belt. "I'm ready."

The others took up their weapons with renewed strength, and the group started westward.

From time to time, the lowland cloud would close on them, the group would stop, someone would confess a stumble, and light would return. Each time, the embarrassment, the sorrow, and the efforts to restore the fallen comrade drained Abigail's energy and soon became tiresome.

Everything about the journey was tiresome. Mile after mile, the drumbeat of footsteps, the endless passing of trees, and the monotony of the lowlands wore on her.

As time dragged on, the landscape began to lose its color. The trees, the sky—even the fruit faded to a dull gray.

The emotional numbness frightened her. Her time in the orchard had taught her that few conditions were more dangerous than feeling nothing. Her soul ached for a spark of color.

"Are we lost?" Levi asked. "I'm not sure we're even going the right way."

"It does indeed seem that we should have arrived by now," Watson said. He looked at Charles. "Don't take offense. But given how seldom you visit the lowlands, perhaps another leader might guide us on a … more direct course."

"How about Adam?" Levi said. "He knows this place. I say he should take the lead."

A rushing sound in the trees caught the group's attention, pulling all eyes upward.

"Is that the wind?" Abigail asked.

The sound grew louder, closer, and turned from a rush to a melodious whistle. A glorious blue cloud appeared above the treetops.

"The Father's colors!" Levi shouted.

The beauty and movement of the cloud washed over Abigail like water in the desert, soothing the burn of her craving for anything to relieve the boredom. Her soul came alive.

The cloud began to move.

"We should follow it," said Levi. "I think the Father is showing us the way out."

"Yeah, I think he's right," Kailyn said.

*****

As the group started toward the cloud, Gibbor tapped Adam on the shoulder and pinged his glasses with a flick of his finger.

Adam adjusted the specs, muttering to himself. "I had forgotten about these."

He studied the cottage piece he had been holding, then stopped short.

"Wait," he said. He adjusted his glasses again and examined the piece more closely. He looked up at the cloud and back to the piece. His face turned white. "Run!"

Chapter 17

Adam turned away from the cloud, but none of the others followed.

Levi pointed up. "I'm pretty sure that's—"

"No, it's not," Adam insisted. "Look." He held up the cottage piece, inscribed with the words, "They have exchanged the colors of the Creator for that of the created."

The group's blank stares prompted an explanation. He pointed to a faint line on the piece. "Do you see that?"

Levi examined it. "See what?"

"I think you're going to have to unfold it for us, Adam," Layth said.

Adam pushed his fingernail into the seam and pulled the piece open. Then he caught two other seams and pealed them back, revealing a drawing. The image was of a man running after a bird with his back to the Father.

He pointed to the cloud. "Those are birds. They are this world's counterfeit of the Father's colors. Theirs are created colors. Created colors are fine when they point us to the Father. But when they distract us from him or serve as a substitute for his colors, the creation becomes a rival to the Creator."

He looked again at the cloud. "That, my friends, is a distraction."

"He's right," Charles said. "Those aren't the Father's colors. Look closely. There's no splendor or majesty. No wisdom, no mercy, no patience. They amuse, but they don't fortify the soul."

Levi reached for the cottage piece. "Let me see." He examined the unfolded piece and looked up again. "Yeah, I see it. Those aren't real colors."

Several birds swooped down and cut through the group, catching everyone's attention, and returned to the flock. As the glorious cloud moved eastward, Adam took a half step in that direction, then squeezed his eyes closed. "No." he shouted, then turned and ran westward.

The group followed.

*****

Gibbor pointed to a battalion of guardians. "Another two hundred just arrived from the high country. Where do you want them?"

Levite surveyed the battled lines. "North end," he said, pointing. "The prince is sending his reinforcements up that way, so we need to strengthen that section."

The line of warriors inched closer to the guardians, both sides on a hair trigger awaiting the signal from their commanders. Pulses raced.

As the friends prepared to make another attempt to bring Abigail across the border, Charles exhorted them. "Keep your mind in the cottage, not on what you see around you. The moment a thought crosses your mind, ask yourself, 'Is it true? Is it noble and right? Pure and lovely? Admirable? Excellent? Praiseworthy? If not, drive it out!"

Horns sounded, and the warriors attacked. The lines collided and the ground shook with the roar of the battle.

Each of the friends glowed purple, wielding their unique weapons. The sounds of ringing steel filled the orchard along with the cries of both warriors and guardians.

Gibbor almost tripped over three warriors who had been flatted by a single stroke from Abigail's sword. He gave an approving nod to Charis before flying off to check on the northern front.

A detachment of warriors managed to separate Watson from the group. None of the friends noticed until Big Red tapped Layth on the shoulder. *To your left—in those trees.*

Layth turned just in time to catch a glimpse of Watson disappearing in into the trees and ran to help him.

Adramelech saw the big man lumbering toward the grove and grabbed Anzu by the shirt, pointing after Layth. "Do something about him!"

Veins popped in Anzu's arms as he took up a rod. "Gladly."

The rabid lieutenant ran and slammed Layth from behind just as he entered the trees. Dust rose and trees shook as the two combatants engaged.

*****

Layth spotted Watson seated on a stone, gazing into nowhere. *I hate it when he gets like this. He's not going to listen to me.*

Layth stopped. His normal eagerness to help a discouraged friend had evaporated. Just walking over and saying a few, simple, uplifting words suddenly felt like an impossible chore. *When Watson wants to be alone, he wants to be alone.*

Layth turned back to the battlefield. But after a few steps, he paused. *Wait. Why is it so hard to say a few words to a friend? This makes no sense.*

*****

Anzu froze. *Did I go too far? Did I give away my—*

A flash of purple lightning exploded from Layth's javelin. Anzu parried the blow and countered. Rage fed Anzu's strength and he rushed Layth in a ferocious assault.

*****

Adramelech, utterly distracted from the battle, stood mesmerized as the cries of Layth's soul and

Anzu's shrieks of horror rose from the tumult within the trees.

An hour passed. The treetops stopped shaking. Adramelech's eyes refused to be pried from the stand of trees. Watching. Watching.

Then, a foot emerged. A leg. Watson strode from the trees, unharmed. Behind him limped Layth, guarding Watson's back.

Adramelech flew to the site of the epic contest. Anzu, rod broken, lay motionless.

*****

Without warning, a powerful craving for grapes arose from deep inside Abigail. She hadn't been thinking about fruit. The desire erupted from nowhere and enveloped her. Memories of the pleasures of fruit flooded her mind, the agony of bondage, forgotten.

The desire strengthened by the moment. It seemed to form itself into an entity of its own, battling Abigail from the inside.

She opened her mouth to call out but had no voice. She looked around frantically. *Where did everyone go?* She ran up a hill for a higher vantage point and looked in every direction. She stood alone—more alone than she had ever been.

Again, she tried to scream. A smoky substance rose from her chest, burned her throat, and spewed from her mouth. The undulating fog swelled and morphed before her. Legs. Arms. A face. A human form. A woman. Blond, curly hair. It was Abigail's own image.

It was like she was looking in a mirror, except the image had a gaping wound in its chest.

"You're my old self." Abigail backed away. "I killed you when I went through the cottage."

The image parted its lips, revealing sharp fangs as it advanced toward Abigail. "You invited me back," it growled through clenched teeth. Claws emerged from its fingers as it crept closer.

Abigail back peddled a few more steps, then stopped. She straightened, leveled her gaze, and drew her sword.

The image drew a sword of its own and lunged in a wild assault.

In a blur, Abigail parried every move. With the speed and skill of a professional swordsman, she wielded the weapon with a single hand, her skin glowing purple.

But as the fight wore on, Abigail's strength faded. Everything in her screamed for fruit. She felt like she would die if she didn't get a taste. Her soul moaned. Her body revolted at the deprivation. Her mind assaulted her.

Still, she fought on, remembering Charles' words about holding, holding, holding.

"Why are you fighting me?" said the image. "You're only hurting yourself. Look! All this fruit—this whole beautiful orchard can be yours. Don't you see? You can still visit the banquet hall while enjoying the orchard. You don't have to give up one for the other."

The glint of Abigail's sword flashed red from an inscription near the tip. *My favor that brings salvation teaches you to say "No" to old passions as you wait for me.* She remembered the blood room. *He died to purchase my purity.*

Abigail faced the vile image and roared. "No!"

"But why deny yourself when you know you can be forgiven? Why not—"

"Why not betray him because I know he will forgive me?" Abigail raised her sword. "Destroy a relationship just because it's possible to rebuild it? That's like saying, 'My leg can heal, so why not break it?'"

She brought the sword down like a flash of lightning across her opponent's thigh, snapping its femur.

Abigail stood above the fallen image with the sword at its throat. "Yes, a broken leg can be healed. But it can also lead to death."

"Strike me," it hissed, "and you will never taste fruit again. I am the only one who can bring you that pleasure—even if it's just once in a while. Remember, there is *no* fruit in the cottage."

Abigail froze. The words "never again" frightened her. Tastes of fruit formed in her mouth. She would *never* enjoy them again?

Then Adam's words jolted her memory. *Will you hesitate? Or will you strike?*

In that instant, the image lunged and tackled Abigail. The thing was trying to climb back into her soul. "You don't have to take any fruit right now," it whispered. "Just leave the door open a crack."

Again, the memories of the orchard's pleasures flooded her mind. Abigail stopped fighting, and her soul began re-absorbing the image.

Just as quickly, words of the cottage spoke in her spirit. *What benefit did you receive at that time from the things you are now ashamed of?* Her skin crawled at a vivid recollection of the snake in her dream.

She took the image by its blond, curly hair and flung it with every reserve of strength within her.

When the image tumbled to a stop, Abigail was already standing over it, sword raised.

"Go ahead and kill me," it said. "I'll be back tomorrow."

"Then I'll kill you again. I'll strike you down every day the rest of my life."

The sword came down so hard it shook the ground. The image dissolved.

Again, powerful cravings arose in Abigail's soul. But this time she craved real food. She longed to be near the Ruler. She wanted to touch the colors. And with those desires came hope. She knew the desires would be fulfilled. For the first time since she had entered the orchard, saying 'no' to the fruit felt like gain, not loss.

Thoughts about fruit, feelings of self-condemnation, the impulse to give up, and self-pity still tried to invade her mind, but she interrupted those thoughts with better ones. *No! Those thoughts are not true, not noble, not right. I will not allow them another moment.* She crowded them out of her mind by relishing the descriptions Watson had given of how he felt when he reconciled with the Ruler after his fall.

She remembered the aromas and flavors of the banquet hall. She recalled some of her best moments in the cottage with the Ruler. She relished memories of the Ruler's wisdom, love, power, patience, mercy, forgiveness, knowledge, tenderness, purity, holiness, majesty, provision, joy, peace, favor—

"Abigail! Down here."

She pushed a pine branch out of the way and scanned the hillside below her until she caught sight of Adam's waving arms. She waved back and started down the hill.

The group met her half way.

"Where were you?" Adam asked. "And why is your sword drawn?"

Abigail looked at the sword in her hand and pushed it into its scabbard. "I …" She looked at her cramping hand and stretched it, then looked over her shoulder.

"Is someone back there?" Kailyn asked.

Adam stepped close and touched her purple hand. "You faced her, didn't you? You struck her down. That's why you made it across so easily."

Abigail looked around. Not a fruit tree in sight. "Where are we?"

Adam smiled. "About a mile west of the orchard. You crossed the border, then ran off. We've been searching for you for the last hour." He put an arm around her. "You did it. You're free."

*****

K-lion and Sol embraced. Charis, Abigail's guardian, danced and sang for joy. The celebration resounded throughout the orchard and the golden city.

Levite smiled for a brief moment when Abigail broke free from the orchard, but a deadly serious expression returned as he set his gaze to the west.

"You're concerned." Big Red observed.

Levite drew a deep breath. He looked back toward the orchard, then again to the west. "It is good to have a small victory. But there is a reason Abigail's rescue came so easily."

Big Red cocked an eyebrow. *Easily?*

"Brace yourself, Red. And see that the others are prepared. There is a greater battle ahead, with much more at stake. This is far from over."

Big Red stood next to him and faced westward. "When you were sent here and an extra five guardians were assigned to Charles, I knew there was more to this operation than meets the eye. Perhaps if we knew what to expect, we could—"

"The Ruler's name is at stake," Levite said. "The hall itself could fall. And the outcome of the battle we are about to face will be determined in great measure by the actions of those two." Levite's eyes rested on Adam and Charles. "Watson as well. All three will be tested beyond anything they have ever endured."

Chapter 18

Adramelech stood at attention before the prince. “We sustained heavy losses, but there are reserves. We could renew the assault within the hour. What are your orders?”

“Our work is finished here. I accomplished what I wanted with Abigail. She’s ready for the next stage in my plan. Leave enough warriors here so the guardians won’t suspect anything. But I want at least two full legions moved to the operation at her banquet hall before she arrives.”

“Under Morax’s command?”

“No. I will handle this operation myself. We will stage in the bronze hall northwest of the cottage. There is no line of sight to the cottage from there, and we now have full control of that hall.”

“As you wish.”

“And Commander …”

“Sir?”

“Do it quietly.”

*****

Abigail stopped and looked back toward the orchard. "I crossed an hour ago?"

Adam drew close. He smiled at a curl that had fallen in front of her eyes and gently swept it back. "After you made it across, I thought you'd be …" He traced her lips with his thumb. "I was hoping to see that smile again."

She looked away.

"What is it, Abigail?"

"I am glad to be free, and I'm grateful—to everyone. But when I think of what this has cost, the danger you all faced …" her eyes teared. "What if one of you had died? I would—"

"Dying to save you would be an honor for any man," Adam said, "which is why we aren't stopping now. Your rescue won't be complete until your smile is restored."

She forced a grin, but it was empty. Even if she could somehow regain her happiness, it would never be like before. Too much had happened.

As they neared the grasslands, the group stopped. A decomposing body lay in the path.

"Just step over it," Levi said. "It's not like it's the first body we've seen with a hole in the chest." Levi seemed puzzled at the group's reaction. "I know it's disgusting to look at, but it's a good thing, right? It means the person was made new, like us. Why are you so—"

Levi caught a glimpse of the man's face. His own face. The group stood in silence.

Levi stepped between the corpse and the group. "Don't look at him. Please, just … don't look."

Charles put a hand on Levi's shoulder. "It's nothing to be embarrassed about Levi. We know that's not what you are anymore. A man is what he is, not what he was."

Levi considered that for a moment, then a smile crept across his face. He nudged the body out of the path with his foot, and the group resumed the journey.

As they walked, Kailyn stepped between Adam and Levi from behind and put an arm around each of them. "So tell us your stories. What was it like going through the cottage?"

"Why ask us?" Levi said. "You've been through it. You know that place a lot better than either of us."

"I know the rooms, but each person's experience in those rooms is unique—especially in the room of delights. I was carried into that room by the Mighty Wind. Is that how it happened for you?"

"I couldn't even get into that room at first," Levi said. "The wind was so fierce on the inside, the door wouldn't open. I threw all my weight against it, and it didn't budge."

Layth let out a hearty belly laugh. *"Your weight*? What weight? I've eaten meals that weighed more than you!"

Levi smiled. "Believe me, Layth, not even you would have been able to open that door, despite your great—"

"Girth?" Layth asked, holding his belly with both hands.

"I was going to say strength. But since you mention it …"

As the friends laughed, Abigail drew close to Adam. "You look happy."

His only reply was a satisfied grin—one Abigail didn't think she had ever seen on his face before.

After a few thoughtful strides, he spoke. "I've had friends before, but not like this. It's hard to describe. To be with people who have fought alongside me, risked their lives for me in battle, picked me up when I was wounded—people who can poke fun at each other without getting offended, and I can just be myself without any fear of rejection. It's like …"

"Like family?"

His smile broadened. He put his arm around her shoulders and pulled her to his side. "Yeah." He filled his lungs. "Like family."

As the group approached the grasslands, Levi ran ahead. But when he reached the tree line, he stopped short.

"What is it?" called Adam.

His silence beckoned the others to jog up to see. When they did, they were also dumbstruck—all except Charles. When the aged server looked out over the valley, he lit up with a smile his face could hardly

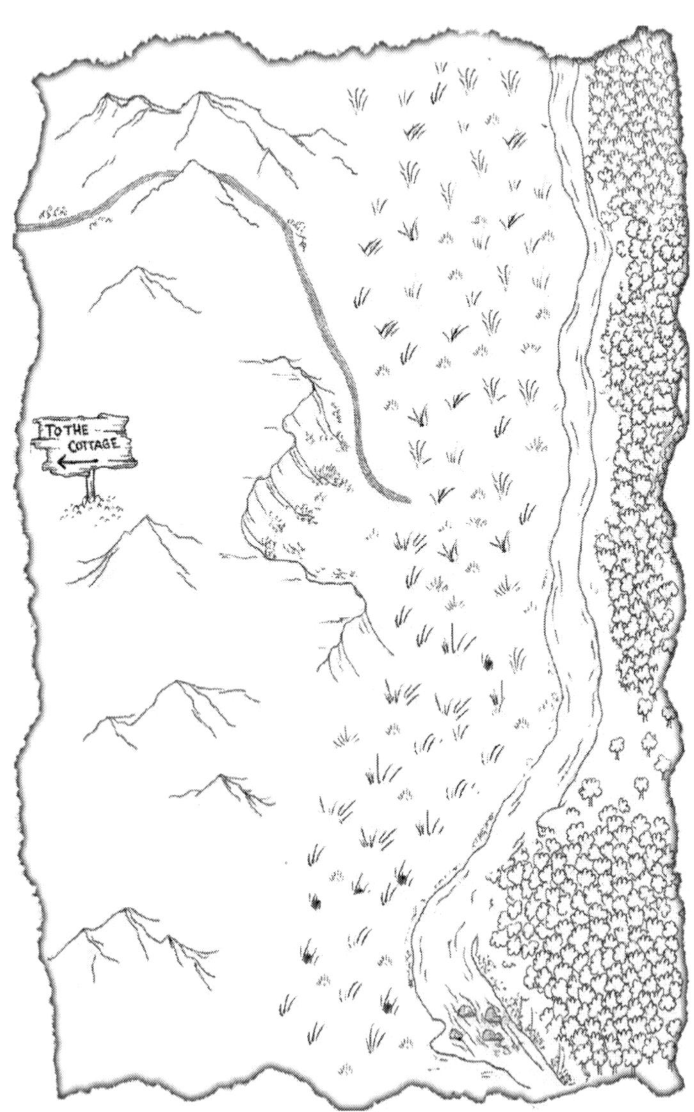
TO THE
COTTAGE

contain. The river now flowed along the edge of the forest, on the east side of the grasslands. It had moved a mile eastward.

The group stood in stunned silence.

"What in the world happened here?" Adam asked.

Still smiling, Charles resumed the journey with renewed energy. "When you see the map room, you'll understand."

*****

Richard Wesley, one of the banquet servers, hadn't stopped running since he left the hall. As he descended the steep slope to the river, he slid more than he ran, sending dirt and rocks tumbling before him.

When the bottom of the valley came into view, he stopped short, almost losing his balance. *Where's the river? Could we have gained territory? At a time like this?*

He scrambled the rest of the way down. It was at the site of the old riverbed where he met the group. Their upbeat greetings quickly gave way to alarm when they saw the look on his face.

"Charles, you have to hurry," Richard pleaded. "The hall is in trouble! Someone got infected and it has spread throughout the hall. They're biting and devouring one another. The family is being torn to shreds, and hardly anyone has been eating."

Charles grimaced. "When I left the hall in your care, I warned you to beware of this."

"I know. I kept watch to the east. But these wolves didn't come from the outside. Charles, it was some of our own servers who gathered a following and became wolves." He gripped Charles' arm. "There's no time for the ridge path. If you don't get back to the hall soon, there might not be a hall when you get back."

Charles cast an anxious look toward the steep path ahead then glanced at Abigail.

"You all go on," Abigail said. "Don't wait for me. I'd slow you down."

"I'm not leaving you alone," Adam said. "They can take care of the wolves. I'll stay with you."

Each of the friends gave Abigail a hug and started up the steep side, Richard leading the way.

*****

When the hall came into view, Charles hardly recognized the place he had spent his life serving. Broken windows, holes in the roof, walls leaning—even the foundations appeared compromised. How could it have become so dilapidated in such a short time?

A splinter pricked his hand as Charles pushed the front door open. Inside, he shivered, as if he had stepped from springtime into a cold, dark winter.

Though almost mealtime, only a handful of people dotted the quiet hall. As more trickled in, they arranged the tables in clusters, each group with their backs to the others.

When the servers brought out the food, few ate. Those who did only nibbled. Everyone appeared malnourished and nursed wounds from too many wolf bites to count.

Charles didn't know where to begin.

As his eyes swept the room, his very life disintegrated before him. Building this family had consumed his every spare moment, all his money, all his thoughts, his skills, his energy—his entire existence had been devoted to making this hall one of the best places in the world to enjoy the Ruler's food. And now …

The Ruler made no appearance during the meal, and when it was over, the hall emptied quickly. Most avoided eye contact with Charles on the way out.

As Hodia approached the exit, Charles pulled her aside. "You know this family as well as anyone. You've been here from the beginning. What happened?"

Her cold, flat tone surprised him. "This is what happens when you neglect the flock. If you want to know why young people in the hall go off to the orchard, just look in the mirror. You don't listen to people. And you run this place like a dictator, as if the hall belonged to you. It doesn't."

A gut punch. Bewilderment silenced him. Hodia, already making her way to the door, didn't seem to want a response anyway.

When all had left, Charles sat at one of the tables and picked at some of the many leftovers. But even he could hardly taste the food. After a few bites, he pushed the plate away and buried his face in his hands. He was glad the people were gone, but at the same time, loneliness haunted him.

What was that? He lifted his head and scanned the room. His eyes landed on the kitchen doors. Someone was in there.

He held his breath and watched. Was the Ruler about to step out and speak to him? Oh, for a simple word of encouragement, an affirming glance—anything to show Charles still had his favor. His desperate eyes locked on the doors, willing them to open.

The longer he watched, the more hope faded, then died. Whatever he heard must have been his imagination.

Had the Ruler forsaken this hall? Had their lamp been snuffed out? Unthinkable, yet every moment the kitchen door remained still, the possibility grew.

Was Hodia right? Had he been an unprofitable servant for the Ruler without realizing it? If that's what he needed to hear from the Ruler, so be it. He just needed to hear *something*.

His gaze refused to let loose of the doors. *Please, let them open. Be comforting or be angry, but come to me.*

The sealed portals stood as giant, motionless stones, and Charles' sobs echoed throughout the desolate space.

*****

Five of Charles' guardians, vastly outnumbered by the warrior host in the room, bravely stood by him, obeying, if not understanding their orders. The sixth conversed with the Ruler in the kitchen.

The stately guardian spoke in a hushed, reverent tone. "I understand the purpose of the test. But why are we not permitted to strengthen Charles' heart? Would it not honor you if he were reassured by your promises?"

"This is a crisis in which I want to strengthen him directly," said the Ruler. "I will lay my hand on his shoulder and bring him comfort that will change him forever. The meal I have prepared for him will nourish every part of his inner man. It will penetrate between joints and marrow. You will soon see what it looks like for a human soul to erupt with delight that dwarfs the cloud of his pain—even as his pain persists."

The guardian's confusion gave way to anticipation. Few things delighted him more than watching the Ruler encourage a saint directly. But traces of confusion remained.

"You're wondering why the delay," said the Ruler. "This will be the greatest meal Charles has ever eaten. But for this kind of food to be digested, he must first have the greatest appetite he has ever had. He must thirst with such desperate pangs that he feels he will die if he does not have a drink. And indeed, he will be on the brink of death. Otherwise his soul would not be able to absorb this food and drink."

The Ruler faced the mighty guardian and gripped both his shoulders. “It is necessary.”

Those last three words the guardian never doubted. The pain the Ruler brought upon his people, while sharp, was never pointless.

Chapter 19

Layth, Kailyn, and Watson sat in wooden chairs around a small kitchen table in Watson's modest home. The fractured banquet hall, visible from the kitchen window, cast a long shadow as the sun drooped westward.

"More tea?" Watson offered.

Layth shook his head.

Kailyn lifted her cup.

"Where is Levi?" she asked as Watson poured. "He should be here. We could use his weapon about now. He makes it so much easier to trust the Ruler. And I'm sure he needs us too. I think he took the hall collapse harder than anyone."

His faith is strong," said Watson, "but uninformed. He has no categories through which to process all that has happened."

"I must say," he added. "My own grasp of the matter is"—he set his cup on the table and stared into it—"inadequate."

Layth shifted in his chair. "It's like Levi said in the battle. The Ruler can be trusted—period. Trusting only when things make sense ain't trusting." He spoke as a man trying to convince himself of his own words. He sighed, leaned back in his chair, and peered out the window toward the hall.

*****

In times like this, Levi wanted to be alone. In truth, he preferred solitude most of the time.

His hike into the hills north of the hall proved rigorous. At the top of the ridge—just west of the clearing where he'd spent that first night with his new friends—he picked a spot overlooking the valley to the east and the banquet halls and cottage to the south. Grateful for the seclusion, he reclined against a log to take in the view and sort his chaotic thoughts.

He had not yet visited the Map Room in the cottage, where the plans and strategies of the Ruler were on display. He had heard bits and pieces, but what he just witnessed seemed exactly opposite of what he understood the Ruler's plans to be. The Ruler's purposes revolved around the banquet halls. If he had the power to prevent it, why would he allow one of his best halls be destroyed?

His swirling confusion about the hall comingled with his deepening sorrow over Abigail. His heart ached for her, certain she would never fully recover. The rescue from the orchard had turned out to be far less than what he had imagined.

"Mind if I join you?"

Startled, Levi turned—and tried not to stare. Before him stood the smallest adult Levi had ever seen. No more than four feet, if that. Yet he carried himself with the confidence of a great man.

The stranger extended his hand. "I'm Doctor Jensen."

"Levi." He shook the man's tiny hand without standing up. *So much for solitude.*

"I don't often run into anyone up here," Jensen said.

It was true. There wasn't much of anything north of the banquet halls, so this spot wasn't on the way to anywhere. If someone came here, it was because he liked to climb, was lost, or wanted to be alone. This man obviously wasn't seeking solitude and seemed to know the place. *Must be a climber.*

"So what brings you up here?" Jensen asked.

"Just needed to get away. I've had a rough couple of weeks." Levi picked up a pinecone and, resting his forearms on his knees, began dismantling it piece by piece. "A friend was trapped in the orchard and a group of us went to rescue her."

"I take it she wouldn't leave?"

"We got her out." Levi bit his bottom lip as he tugged at an especially stubborn scale on the cone. It broke free, and he flicked it skyward. It rose, stalled, then plummeted downward into a rock pile below. "Thing is, she's different now. She used to be a really happy person, but now she's so down on herself. I don't know what to do."

"That's tough," Jensen acknowledged, taking a seat beside Levi. "I know exactly what that's like. I went through the same thing myself not long ago."

*****

Levite, Levi's guardian, gripped his sword when he saw Doctor Jensen approach, empowered by one of Adramelech's lieutenants. *Lucius!*

A stench wafted from behind him, and Levite spun. Four more warriors. He didn't know them, but he guessed they were also high-ranking warriors. Each the size of Lucius or larger.

Surrounded, Levite turned slowly. Every fiber of his being tensed. Lucius himself would have been a handful. But four lieutenants at once …

At first, Levite was surprised that such a force would be sent against a man like Levi. But then again—he glanced at Levi's face, the face of a man racked by compassion for Abigail. The combination of faith and compassion posed a threat that attracted attention at the highest levels. Clearly, the prince had not given up on Abigail, and anyone who might have a hand in her restoration remained in his crosshairs.

If Lucius' presence was surprising, his strategy was anything but. The same, age-old tactic. In a time of sorrow, isolate and deceive. And if the subject's faith can't be shaken, misdirect it through confusion and deception, trapping him in a stronghold. Lucius' specialty.

"You *went* through the same thing—past tense?" Levi asked. "Sounds like you recovered. How did you do it?"

"There were a number of factors. But I think the biggest was learning to forgive myself."

Unseen by the men, a stone wall formed behind Levi. As Dr. Jensen spoke, the wall grew, rising to the height of the treetops with a thickness the span of a man's outstretched arms. Then steel plating grew out of the ground and overplayed the wall on both sides.

Levite had seen this stronghold before. He drew himself to his full height and raised his sword. Normally he wouldn't consider this a winnable fight, but allowing Levi to be imprisoned in the self-love stronghold—he would be cut to pieces before letting that happen.

Lucius shouted at Dr. Jensen. "Keep talking about self-forgiveness. Make him believe Abigail can absolve herself. Keep his focus off the Father."

The wall began to curve around Levi, now behind and on both sides. Levite flew take hold of Levi and pull him out before the wall closed him in completely.

But Lucius' blow came so fast, Levite didn't see it coming. It caught the side of his helmet and sent him reeling. He recovered, and Lucius lowered his sword, daring a counter strike.

Levite rushed Lucius, causing him to step back and brace for the collision. But at the last second, Levite cut sideways to Levi's side and whispered in his ear.

*****

Levi looked up from his pinecone. “You forgave *yourself*? How does absolving yourself restore a broken relationship with the Father?”

Jensen stared blankly, as if it had never occurred to him that forgiveness was the restoration of a relationship.

Understandable, Levi thought. *Guess I never realized what forgiveness was before the cottage either.*

Jensen tried again. “I .. uh … my point is that the Father isn’t angry. He is full of love and compassion, not anger or revenge. I came out of my depression when I realized that what I thought was the Father’s anger was just me angry at myself. The Father never gets angry with us.”

“You speak as if you know the Father personally.”

“Know him? Oh … well … I, um …”

Levi continued. “When you say the Father never gets angry, are you saying he gives commands but doesn’t care if we obey them?”

Jensen straightened his shirt. “I’m just saying it’s the mountain people, not the Father, who get uptight about eating fruit. Why would the Father care if someone nibbles an orange? How does that hurt him? He wants us to be happy, and if it takes a little fruit here and there for me to be happy, the Father understands. What he wants to protect us from is not fruit. It’s unhappiness and low self-esteem.”

*****

All four warriors seized Levite and threw him backward. Then one blocked the stronghold opening, which was collapsing by the second, while the other three pinned Levite to the ground.

Lucius clamped his huge hand around Levite's throat.

Levite pulled at Lucius' fingers, but the battle-hardened spirit only grinned and gripped even tighter. Levite slammed the butt of his sword against Lucius' face twice, but the other two warriors took hold of his arm and twisted the sword of out his grasp.

Levite shouted. *Remember the mirror room!*

*****

Levi tilted his head. "*Self*-esteem? When I had high esteem for myself, that's when I was at my worst. But when the Ruler took me through the cottage, he showed me real life and joy came through esteeming *him* more highly. And esteeming others more than myself."

"Ah, yes, it is important to love others. But you can never love others properly until you learn to love yourself. That's what the Ruler meant when he said, 'Love your neighbor as yourself.'"

*****

Lucius laid a dagger at Levite's throat and grinned.

But a blow from behind struck Lucius in the side and he folded. The other two warriors left Levite and rose to face the newcomer.

Levite smiled. There was no mistaking the ring of Big Red's sword. And between him and the warriors stood not only Big Red, but Sol and K-lion as well.

*****

"Hi guys." Levi stood to greet Layth, Watson, and Kailyn. He was glad to see them—unusually glad. He felt something like relief, which was strange. It wasn't like the little guy was any threat. With a sideways tip of his head he said, "This is—"

"Dr. Jensen," Watson said.

"Oh, you've met?"

Watson's tone was grim. "He is the leader of the littles ones."

Watson faced Jensen. "I couldn't help overhearing your theory about how the command to love others is really a command to love ourselves. Tell me, if that's the case, how is it that selfish people commit murder?"

"Or leave their wives for another woman?" Kailyn added. "Wasn't it you who counseled Alexander to leave me because the Father wanted him to be happy? He did a great job loving himself. But was he loving me?"

"No one needs to learn self-love." Watson added. "People already love themselves. We are born that way."

"A lot of people hate themselves," Jensen objected.

"It may feel that way," Watson said. "However, even in times of self-loathing or self-harm, there is no one you serve, protect, or feel more pity for than yourself."

Levi stood and took a step forward. "Yeah, that's how it was for me. I hurt a lot of people when I was looking out for number one."

*****

Just as Levi stood and with a nudge from his guardian, stepped forward, the two ends of the circular wall met, sealing the enclosure and missing Levi by inches.

Lucius cursed and barked an order at the others. "Guard the stronghold!"

But Watson kept pounding at it. "Loving the Father and others is only possible when we disregard the esteem we have for ourselves. To follow the Ruler, one must deny himself—not love himself."

A large crack spider webbed along one side of the fortress and the structure tilted to one side.

Layth joined the assault. He couldn't see the growing prison cell threatening to entrap Levi but was well aware of the danger of spiritual strongholds. He lifted a massive cottage piece and hurled it at the stronghold, reciting the inscription as he threw it. "Do nothing out of selfish ambition or vain conceit, but in humility consider others more important than yourselves. Love is not self-seeking."

Watson turned to Levi. "Abigail's sorrow is appropriate. The Ruler taught us that when we do evil, we must rend our hearts. We should grieve, mourn, and wail and change our laughter to mourning and our joy to gloom."

Never had Levite seen the self-love stronghold reduced so quickly to a pile of rubble.

Dr. Jensen gasped and looked up, then to all sides. He held his arms out in defense against an invisible threat. "What was that?"

"What was what?" Levi said.

"You didn't feel it? It was like … the air … it … it moved."

Lucius' face turned white. The other three warriors nearly trampled one another in their panicked retreat. Lucius also backed away, shouting at Jensen. "Get out now. Run. You're not safe. *Run!*"

*****

Jensen's alarm melted to a look of sadness.

"Hey!" said Kailyn, pointing at the ground beneath Jensen. "Look!"

Layth and Watson smiled. Levi gazed in astonishment at Jensen's feet, which spanned at least an inch longer than the tracks he'd left on his approach.

Kailyn stepped close to Dr. Jensen and gently lifted his chin with her fingers. "What you're feeling is good. It's the kind of sorrow that pushes you toward life instead of death. It's the early stages of humility. I know you don't believe in the Great Wind, but why not come with us to the cottage? You can meet the Ruler, hear him out, and decide for yourself."

Jensen stood silent for a long moment. The corners of his mouth crept upward, then reversed into a frown. He lifted his eyes and opened his mouth but closed it before speaking. Wrinkles overtook his forehead, then smoothed. His gaze clouded. "I … I don't think so."

With that, he set out down the eastward path.

Kailyn stood motionless for a full two minutes, watching him.

"I don't think he's coming back, Kailyn," Layth said.

"But he felt the wind," she said, still not taking her eyes off Jensen.

"It's *Jensen*," Layth said. "He's not going to—"

"Just—" she put up a hand toward Layth and kept watching. "Come on," she whispered, as if Jensen would somehow sense her call. "You know something's happening inside you. Just stop and come back."

Finally, he disappeared from sight.

Kailyn wiped a lone tear from her eye and faced her friends. "It will be dark soon. We should probably head back down."

"I'm ready," Levi said.

Layth nudged Levi as they started down the trail. "What were you doing up here anyway?"

"I don't know. I just …" He shook his head. "Did Abigail make it back? How's she doing?"

"She is …" Watson cleared his throat. "It's hard for her."

"You're her brother," Levi said. "Surely you know what it would take to cheer her up. We have to do *something*."

"We do indeed. But cheer is not what she needs right now. Do you remember when you crawled out of the mirror room in the cottage?"

"How do you know I crawled? I never told—"

Watson smiled. "Everyone crawls. It is the only way out of that room. Anyone so proud as to remain standing must stay until their knees finally give way."

"So … what? You're saying Abigail's going to have to go in there and look in the mirrors before facing the Father?"

"Not if she is already humble and broken. That is why her sorrow now is a good thing. But we must be careful. The prince will endeavor to use her sorrow against her by turning it into the sorrow that leads to death rather than the kind that will drive her to the Father. We must keep her focus on the promise room so she does not lose heart."

Levi had mixed memories of the floorless promise room. On one hand, he recalled the comfort, rest, hope, and joy he experienced there. But just as vivid was the image of a woman plummeting into the bottomless abyss when she refused to trust the Ruler.

"The promise room is great if you can make it through," Levi said, "But what if Abigail's not up to it?"

"It is never a question of ability. Only willingness. When people do not receive what is promised, it is not because the bar is so high that they are *unable* to meet it, but because it is so low that they are *unwilling*. Humility is agonizing to the proud heart."

"Makes sense," Levi said. "But I still hate seeing her like this. She's miserable. I just want her to feel a little better about herself."

"True repentance is excruciating, but nothing like the misery that falls upon the unrepentant. The only path to joy is to return to the giver of joy. And that path must cross the valley of contrition. What Abigail needs is to see the Father's colors. I assure you, feeling good about the Father feels better than feeling good about oneself."

*****

The dilapidated hall loomed before Abigail like a warehouse of shame. "I can't go in there. I can't face these people after what I've done. And the way I look—I just … I can't."

She turned away, but Adam held her. "Your friends are in there. Layth and Kailyn risked their lives for you. So did Levi. And he hardly knows you."

"They came for me when the Ruler sent them, but when they saw me, they all felt the same thing—disgust. I saw it in their eyes. I even see it in yours sometimes."

"No you don't. Never for a single moment. Every glimpse of you only deepens my love for you." He pointed to the door. "And I know there are plenty of others in there who will be thrilled to see you."

Eyes downcast, Abigail was reminded of the worst of her deformities—her feet. They had withered to the size of a lowlander's feet. And the putrid stains of the orchard could be seen through the holes in her shoes.

She covered one foot with the other and lifted her face back to Adam, hoping his gaze hadn't followed hers. "Adam, you don't understand. I have nothing to offer anymore. I used to bring people joy, but now …" She shook her head.

"You feel … colorless?"

She covered her face and nodded.

"The colors you had before—where did you get them?"

She looked toward the hall.

"So the only thing you ever had to offer was what the Ruler gave you?"

Again, she gave a silent nod.

"So if you want to have something to offer, and the source of all colors is in that hall, isn't that where you want to be?"

He moved close and caressed her cheek. "You will find your joy again." He took her face in both hands. "The Ruler designed you to wear that smile. He wants to see it again even more than I do, which is saying something."

"I know I need the Ruler," she said. "But I can't be around people right now. Let me just go to the cottage and meet with him there."

"But isn't it through his people that the Ruler dispenses his love? And isn't it through loving them that you receive the most joy? If you want your smile back, I don't see any other way."

He pointed to the entrance. "Everything you need is in there—the Ruler, his food, his family."

"And wolves," she added. "What if they—"

"Even if there are wolves, if the Ruler is there, and it's where he serves his food, where else can you go?"

He took a step toward the door and held out a hand to her. "Any wolf that wants to bite you will have to go through me first."

She drew a deep breath, wiped her eyes, and took his hand. He pushed the door open, and they stepped into the hall.

Chapter 20

"Miss Abigail! You're back!" A young girl ran across the hall and jumped into Abigail's arms. "I missed you so much!"

Abigail squeezed the girl tight. "I missed you too Libby."

Tears welled up in Abigail's eyes when moments later the girl's mother and several others greeted her, along with Kailyn and Watson.

When Hodia approached, Abigail thought, *Adam was right. What was I so afraid of? They still love me.*

"Hodia! How have you … been?" Her words trailed off when Hodia walked right by without even meeting Abigail's eyes.

Hodia took the girl's mother by the elbow. She whispered something, and the mother shot Abigail a shocked glance, grabbed her daughter's hand, and cut a hard path through the crowd away from Abigail.

The gnawing abyss of despair reopened inside Abigail and swallowed the glimmers of hope that had sparked. The pain was so sharp she touched her stomach to see if there was a physical wound.

A firm, gentle hand warmed her shoulder and Charles' fatherly voice calmed her. "It will be a mixed response, I'm sad to say. Those who remember their own bondage in the orchard will celebrate your return. Those who have forgotten their former bondage, or who imagined theirs to have been a bondage of lesser shame, will tolerate your presence. And those who are still in bondage but don't realize it will"—he motioned toward Hodia and the other woman—"do that."

Abigail turned toward the door but Charles caught her arm. "Be patient with them, Abigail. Remember when you had to raise the sword against your old self to escape the orchard? That's the same battle these people are in right now. Every soul in this hall will be tested."

She recalled how difficult that moment had been. She had no idea how much her heart cherished her own evil until she had to deliver that death blow and it felt like it was she who died.

Shame and sorrow gave way to compassion. Those people with their backs to her, despising her—they were trapped in the same prison she had just escaped. And winning their freedom would prove just as costly as hers. She ached for them. She wanted to help them, as the others had helped her. But without her weapon, what could she do?

A small gathering formed around one of the servers. Abigail couldn't make out what they were saying, but none of them looked happy. The group became increasingly animated until the server finally nodded and crossed toward Adam. He positioned himself between Adam and Abigail with his back to Abigail.

"Welcome Adam," said the impeccably-dressed server. "Perhaps I could get you a jacket?"

Adam's dirty, tattered clothes definitely stood out, as did Abigail's equally grubby attire.

*****

Seven warriors rocketed down from the ceiling, swords trained on Adam. Gibbor struck like lightning. He slashed through five of the diving warriors with one stroke of his sword and finished the other two on the return sweep.

A moment later, fifty warriors encircled him. Gibbor walked in a slow circle around Adam, glaring at each one. "Who's first?"

The warriors exchanged glances. None advanced.

Gibbor singled out one, pinned him with a hard stare, and moved toward him. That warrior wilted, stepped back, and turned to flee. But before he could make his retreat, he found himself facing the prince of darkness.

The prince's eyes flashed fire.

The warrior wheeled around and flew toward Adam, followed by the rest.

Gibbor stationed himself in front of Adam and unleashed his fury, cutting down wave after wave of attacks. Three huge warriors dropped from above.

Gibbor sent all three flying with a single stroke, still fending off the frontal attack.

But soon those surging from the rear overtook Adam. "Remember this?" shouted one of the warriors. He replayed Adam's first meeting with the Great Ones.

*****

Adam regarded the impressive man before him and noted his perfectly tailored suit. It was the suit, and the suit alone, Adam thought, that made the man impressive.

Everyone else in the remarkable crowd displayed equally flattering clothes. He suddenly felt naked in his torn and stained garments. *I stick out like a sore thumb in this crowd.*

A memory flashed into his consciousness—a memory so vivid it seemed to be playing out before his eyes. He stood before the Great Ones, longing for their approval more than anything in the world.

Next came recollections of years in the golden city when he longed for acceptance in that world but never really found it. Always an outsider.

Then came the scene of his first visit to the banquet hall when he so desperately wanted to fit in.

Memory after memory of times he had been rejected, neglected, or marginalized cut into his soul.

*****

Stinging heat ripped across Gibbor's back. He spun and snapped the attacker's sword with his free arm. But another warrior cut his leg. Gibbor kicked past him and smashed the butt of his sword into the face of another. Again, a shot of pain torched his side. Then another. *There are ... too many.*

The attack on Adam was equally fierce, and Gibbor saw Adam's spirit begin to wilt. In a surge of resolve, he thrust several warriors from his back, and through searing pain, pressed toward the two dark menaces speaking into Adam's ear. He ran his sword through one and flung the other away by his hair.

In an instant, another cloud of warriors descended on him.

He managed to speak one sentence into Adam's mind before the dark mob pulled him away. *Mind your feet.*

As he was being dragged away, Gibbor shouted to Adam, "Greatness in the eyes of men is not greatness!"

*****

Glancing down, Adam saw his feet shrinking. Then he noticed the servers' feet. They were as small as a lowlander's. *Why do I care about what they think?*

"Sir?" said the server.

Adam looked up from his feet and accepted the jacket from the server. "Thank you." He slung it over his shoulder. "What do you have for Abigail?"

The server took Adam's elbow, pulled him a few steps away, and lowered his voice. "I don't think the people are quite ready."

"Ready for what?" Adam said in full voice.

The man adjusted his collar and cleared his throat. "Disobedience to the Ruler cannot be taken lightly. When there has been a failure of this magnitude, the person needs to understand the damage she has done. If she is simply welcomed back with open arms, without any consequences, what does that say to our children?"

"That you have a forgiving heart like the Ruler?"

The server smiled, which seemed calculated to hide his increasing discomfort. "Of course we all forgive her. But there are consequences for what she did."

"Are there consequences for other evils like, say, unforgiveness? Or self-righteousness? Or maybe pride? How about gossip?"

The server's face reddened. "That's not the same thing. I'm disappointed in you Adam. You seem to think what she did is a small matter. It makes me wonder if you've been eating just as much fruit as Abigail."

By now the people who had spoken to the server surrounded Adam.

He braced himself. *Here it comes.*

But the rebuke he'd expected didn't come. "We want to welcome you, Adam," a man said. "Congratulations on escaping the orchard. We're honored to have you."

"Oh, uh, thanks. I—"

A woman hugged him. "We're so glad you're here. I know it can feel overwhelming when you're new. But all you have to do is be yourself."

These people had never even met him, yet they embraced him like a brother. For the first time in his life he … *belonged.*

He found himself walking with the group as they migrated back to their table.

Once seated, a man slid a plate in front of Adam. "Dig in."

Adam eyed the mound of food on the plate. This had been that man's meal. He marveled. Sharing your own plate—that's not the sort of thing you do with a guest. That's something … *brothers* might do.

As the group at the table laughed, joked, and exchanged stories, Adam leaned back in his chair. Never had he felt more at home—like he'd been part of this group for years. All his life, Adam had to *earn* a place in people's lives. But these people—they'd just met him and—"

"I'm curious," said one of the women. "Hodia saw Abigail eating grapes in the orchard. You were with her, right? What other kinds of fruit did she eat?"

"Other kinds? Well, um, I don't—"

"Poor thing," said the woman who had hugged him. "She used to be so beautiful." She shook her head, then looked back at Adam and smiled. "But we believe in restoration. In time, if she proves herself, she will be welcomed back."

"In time? What does that mean—she's on some kind of … probation?"

The woman laughed. "Oh no. Nothing like that. It's just that when someone does what … well, you know … when someone goes that far, we can't pretend nothing happened. It takes time."

Adam studied each face at the table. "Time? I thought if a person returned to the Father—"

"Would you say it was because of her influence that you ended up walking out the last time you were here?" the server asked. "And when you were in the lowlands with her, did she …"

Distracted by the war raging in his heart, Adam didn't catch the rest of what he said. He felt pressure to agree with their attitude toward Abigail. Or to at least keep quiet. His place in this family suddenly felt … tenuous—like it may be in jeopardy if he associated himself with Abigail.

"Just look at her," said the server. "Does she look to you like she belongs here?"

Adam turned in his seat and studied Abigail as if sizing her up for the first time.

Without taking his gaze from her, he replied. "When I look at her, I see a daughter of the builder of the cottage and a sister of the Ruler of the kings of the earth. I see royalty." Adam faced the group. "And I see a fearless friend who risked her life to save Kailyn's when she was being attacked by wild animals. I see a woman who can change the course of a man's life simply by her smile."

"Most of all," he added, now locking his gaze on the server, "I see *humility*."

The server scoffed, then stood and left the table. Adam jumped to his feet and stepped in front of him.

"Do you remember the Father's words? 'I live in a high and holy place, but also with him who is contrite and lowly in spirit, to revive the spirit of the lowly, and to revive the heart of the contrite'?"

The server's look of confusion made Adam wonder if the man had ever even been to the cottage.

He continued. "The Father lives in two places: in the cottage, and in the humble, repentant heart. The prince of darkness also lives in two places: in the lowlands and"—he fingered the man's chest—"in the proud heart."

Adam started to walk away but then turned back. "And if you people are thinking I'm no better than Abigail"—he tossed the jacket back to the server—"that's the one thing you got right."

The prince of darkness had both hands pressed firmly against the man's ears, so none of Adam's words penetrated. He had also hardened the others' hearts so thoroughly that Adam's words landed like seeds on a paved road.

Adam strode toward the kitchen doors and hopped up on the platform. "I have something to say," he shouted. The milling crowd hushed.

"Some of you are offended that two malnourished people have just come from the orchard to visit your banquet hall. I'm new to all this, so perhaps you can tell me—what is the purpose of the banquet hall? Is it not to feed the malnourished? I was told the sole requirement for entry was appetite, which we have. Do you?"

He scanned the crowd. A dropping pin would have startled everyone. Adam lowered his voice. "Perhaps I'm wrong. I hope I am."

Charles approached the platform. "Looks like it's dinnertime," Adam said. "I guess we'll see who's hungry and who's just … pretending."

Chapter 21

Watson sat close to his sister as he watched Charles Baxter rise and make his way to the platform. Murmurs rippled through the crowd.

Layth, seated on the other side of Watson, leaned close and whispered. "This is the most important meal he'll ever serve."

Watson had been thinking the same thing. Which menu items would Charles select on an occasion like this?

A hush fell over the crowd, all eyes fixed on Charles Baxter.

"It's no secret," he began. "This hall is divided. And right now, each faction expects me to serve up a meal that will taste sweet to them and bitter to the others. Just remember—I will be serving only the Ruler's food, nothing else."

A wave of whispers swept the hall.

"The menu today has been served before—by the Ruler himself in a situation quite similar to ours. It has been celebrated as one of the most delicious meals he ever served. Yet some palates at the time found it exceedingly bitter. I hope none of you will find it bitter, though I fear some will. If so, please know the Father has a special word of life just for you."

More stirrings.

"A father had two sons, the younger rebellious, the elder compliant. When the troublesome boy reached adulthood, he abandoned the family, broke the father's heart, and disappeared into the orchard."

Gasps sounded as people realized he was telling a story about someone who did exactly what Abigail had done.

Many nodded in approval. Whispers spread. "Charles has never singled someone out like that before."

"She deserves it," someone else muttered.

Abigail dropped her head to the table and covered it with her arms. Watson stroked her hair.

Abigail spoke softly. "It's true—what they are saying about me. It's all true, and even more. I loved the fruit more than I loved the Ruler. I—"

"You don't have to do this!" said Levi, rising to his feet. "This is none of their business. It's between you and the Ruler. All you're doing is making yourself more miserable."

Layth put a hand on Levi's arm.

Levi glared at him, then lowered himself back into his seat.

Watson spoke to the whole table. "What Abigail is doing is beautiful. True repentance is a powerful internal force and it *will* come out. It must vent itself at the eyes by weeping, and at the mouth by confessing. Just as the body will expel poison from the stomach, confession does the same for the soul. That is why the Ruler instructs us to confess our sins to one another so that we may be healed."

Watson looked at Levi. "Remember what it was like for you when you first repented? You did the same thing. When a man's confession runs through him like water through a pipe, leaving no wounds on the heart, it remains superficial. Many declare resolutions to change when they are in the throes of bondage, but those vows dissolve once the hard consequences of evil are removed. True change of heart continues to build and does not relent until it drives one to full reconciliation with the Father and his family."

"Besides," he added, "look at the forgiveness and comfort she is receiving from the people at this table. Her public confession is allowing for public restoration and expressions of love. The Ruler wants her to feel his love through his people."

"I know you're right," Levi mumbled. Then he raised an arm toward Charles. "But does he have to humiliate her in front of everyone by telling a story like that?"

Layth and Watson, who had both enjoyed this same meal before, smiled.

"Just listen," Layth said.

They all turned back toward the platform just as Charles described the wayward son hitting bottom. "Ravaged by the consequences of his evil, penniless and lost, he became desperate."

Charles paused and looked into the faces of each listener until he had everyone's full attention. So riveted were they that only those at Abigail's table noticed the Ruler slip in through a side door, take Abigail by the hand, and lead her outside.

"Now," Charles said, "what should that son have done at that point?"

"Leave the orchard!" someone shouted.

"No!" thundered Charles. "That is not the solution. He was malnourished, broke, and dying. What good would come from simply leaving the orchard? He would simply die somewhere else."

Charles stared the crowd down until dead silence engulfed the room, then spoke softly. "No. The only way out is for him to *return home to his Father,* which is exactly what he did. And when the Father saw him, what do you think happened?"

*****

Outside the hall, Abigail trembled. "Where are we going?" She couldn't bring herself to meet the Ruler's eyes as they began walking.

"It is time for you to face the Father."

Her lungs turned to stone. She had given much thought to what she would say to the Father when she saw him. Profoundly aware of how she had provoked his displeasure, she felt soiled on the inside—a loathsome, offensive bit of debris. *All I can do is appeal to his compassion and beg for mercy.*

Would the Father take the Mighty Wind from her for good, as he did with Alexander? Or would he have mercy? And if he forgave her, would it be too much for her to ask him to restore her smile? If the deformities of her body remained, she could live with that, but she longed for her lost joy.

Once inside the cottage, Abigail's humble posture allowed her to pass beyond the mirror room without the agony of seeing her image.

"Thank you," she whispered.

Her relief, however, dissolved when the dreadful command sounded from the Ruler's lips. "Take off your shoes."

"Oh no. Please my Lord—not that. Don't make me show my feet." How could she expose her worst ugliness to the Ruler when she could hardly bear to look at them herself?

"This is the only way, Abigail. If you do not remove your shoes, I will not accompany you into the throne room. You will be on your own, and you will be consumed."

Ice ran through her veins. The thought of going anywhere without the Ruler was intolerable. The thought of approaching the Father without him, unimaginable. She pulled her shoes from her feet but kept her eyes fixed on the Ruler.

As the stench from her feet filled the room, shame tortured her soul. In this moment, reality seized her—

even if she got her smile back, it would be nothing like before, lit by purity and innocence. She would be forever deformed. Regret would remain her eternal companion.

The Ruler removed his glorious robes and, wearing only a loincloth, wrapped a towel around his waist. He knelt before Abigail with a basin of water and began cleaning her feet.

The residue from the orchard had seeped underneath the top layers of her skin. The Ruler scrubbed harder and harder until she screamed in pain. "Stop! Please. It hurts. Please stop."

The Ruler paused and looked up at her with a look that reminded her of his previous words. *I will not accompany you.* Abigail took a deep breath, closed her eyes, and nodded for him to continue.

The torture seemed to stretch for hours.

At last, the Ruler dried her feet with a towel, stood, and dressed himself.

The skin on her feet now shone like a baby's, the deformities gone. Her sweet fragrance scented the room.

"Now," said the Ruler, "it is time."

The moment they entered the throne room, Abigail collapsed on the floor in a river of tears. It was the closest she had ever been to the throne.

She had been in human courtrooms and was intimidated, but nothing like this. She sensed if she so much as looked at the Father, she would not survive the brilliance of his glory.

Lying prostrate, she felt the purity of the transparent gold floor radiating into her.

Then the floor shook. Thud! Was it the mighty Judge's gavel? *Boom*, another impact. Then another. *Boom, boom, boom*. The impacts grew louder—and closer. She lifted her head a split second before the Father touched her.

The sound had been the Father running to her. She glimpsed his huge smile as he raised her to her feet, then wrapped her up in his arms, lifting her off the ground. She almost lost her breath as he held her in the tightest, longest embrace she had ever received. Abigail's shoulder was wet with the Father's tears. Pulling her face against his, the Father's voice cracked. "Welcome home, Abigail!"

Chapter 22

Sol monitored the reactions of the various factions as Charles continued the story. They all seemed fine with the part about the younger brother leaving the orchard and returning home, but when Charles described the exuberant response of the Father and the details of the celebration that followed, many shifted in their seats.

Then, the words that set off the storm. "None of that is the point of the story," Charles said. "The main course is what happened next. It was the response of the older brother. He didn't celebrate. In fact, he was angry. He asked the father, 'Why should he get a party? Why not me? I never did the things he did.'"

"Now listen carefully," Charles continued. "The reason the Ruler gave us this story was to show us that the older brother's response was exactly the *opposite* of the father's."

Gibbor tensed as he saw heart after heart recoil at Charles' concluding words.

"Each one of you has had an opportunity to discover something about your own heart when you saw Abigail today. Answer honestly—is your heart like the father's? Or are you like the older brother?"

The Mighty Wind blew, and not gently. It began above, near the high ceiling. A clap of thunder rattled the building. More than a clap. The deafening boom rolled and echoed, growing louder. The hall's foundation shifted, shaking the floor. People's mouths gaped, but their shrieks could not be heard over the roar of the Mighty Wind.

"Look," said Layth, pointing to cracks forming at the center of the ceiling.

Then, silence, and stillness. The quaking, the chaos—it all came to an instant stop.

The front door opened, and blinding light filled the room. As the people's eyes adjusted, gasps echoed through the hall. In the doorway stood three figures—the Ruler, the Father, and, between them, Abigail. The Father held Abigail's right hand, the Ruler her left.

Abigail's face couldn't be seen. It was turned to the Ruler, whose ancient scars seemed strangely fresh.

The Father looked over his family and with a beaming smile and a voice filled with a father's pride said, "Behold, my daughter!"

Abigail turned to the people and her face lighted with a smile that infused the entire hall with energy. Some stood in stunned amazement. A woman ran to Abigail and threw her arms around her. Many others in the room embraced one another.

Charis leaned in to Gibbor. "Such a smile has never been seen in this hall."

Gibbor pointed. "Look at the Father."

"Yes, I see it. Her smile is identical to his."

The warriors in the hall stumbled into one another, blinded by the light of Abigail's smile.

*****

Abigail sought out the woman who had rejected her earlier. "I have to tell you what happened," Abigail said.

As she relayed the story of her meeting with the Father, the woman's cold face warmed. By the end, both their eyes were moist with tears.

"I have something I need to confess," the woman said. "Me too," said another woman who had joined them.

Soon a stream of confessions flowed from broken hearts throughout the hall. Abigail embraced those confessing, reminded them of promises, spoke of her gratitude to the Father, and raved about the Ruler's excellencies, her smile beaming brighter and brighter the more she spoke.

One by one, traces of her smile emerged on faces throughout the hall. And with each glimmer of joy she sparked in others, her own smile brightened.

Within an hour, smiles radiated from many. About a quarter of the crowd, Gibbor guessed. Despite the frowns of the others, laughter broke out among the minority. Then singing.

Her joy was lost, her beauty marred
Trapped by fruit, in bondage barred
But now the smile of glory glows
The Father's face in hers he shows

The Father roared in laughter. Then he squeezed Abigail's hand. "Where is all your self-loathing, daughter?"

She requited his squeeze, then dropped to one knee and bowed her head. "My thoughts of myself mean nothing to me. Your hand on me is … everything!"

"Do you all understand?" said the Father. "The greater the evil, the more profound and incomprehensible the forgiveness. The darker the picture of failure the prince painted in Abigail's mind, the more exuberant her love for the one who carried that evil for her and now accepts her."

The Ruler turned to Abigail. "You feared your smile would never be the same as before. You're right. The smile now radiating from your soul is to your old smile what a sunrise is to an ember. The rise from the blackness of the tunnels to the light of the cottage, from the agonies of regret to the purity of a cleansed conscience, from the despair of bondage to freedom to delight in the good—the deeper the darkness from which I draw a soul, the brighter my colors shine in her love."

He turned to the crowd. "The very life of my Father will pour out upon all who love her smile."

*****

Hodia hated Abigail's smile. Seated with some like-minded friends, she whispered, "Look at her. She's acting like nothing even happened. For her to be grinning like that after the shame she brought on this entire hall …"

Moved by an impulse she didn't understand, Hodia rose and made her way near a side door. Friends from her table also stationed themselves at other doors along the back. In a synchronized action, then they flung all the doors open.

Hundreds of warriors poured through each door. The guardians' swords flashed, and the hall erupted in the clash of good and evil.

Leaving Gibbor and the others to his generals, the prince focused on the people who despised Abigail's smile. He would not delegate the task of stoking the fires of self-righteousness, pride, and anger.

Sol fought his way through a cloud of warriors as Watson cut a path to Hodia, who was gathering a following.

As Watson approached her, he stood toe to toe with the prince of darkness. Sol took a deep breath. *He has no idea.*

"Hodia, stop!" Watson waved an arm toward the crowd. "You are destroying this place. And the Ruler has warned us—if anyone destroys his hall, the Ruler will destroy her!"

"*I'm* destroying it? I'm not the one who went traipsing off into the orchard—"

Watson sheathed his warning dagger and drew a larger one—rebuke. "This is how we know who the children of the Father are and who the children of the prince of darkness are—anyone who does not love her sister is a child of darkness."

"You're calling me a child of darkness?"

"You are behaving like Cain, who belonged to the evil one and murdered his brother. And why did he murder him? Because his own actions were evil and his brother's were righteous. Anyone who hates her sister is a murderer, and you know that no murderer has eternal life."

The prince staggered and dropped to one knee.

Hodia glared at Abigail across the room.

Abigail wilted.

The Ruler cupped Abigail's face in his hands. "Look at me. Remember the Father's approval. You have his favor—and mine. Nothing else matters. She who kneels before me can stand before anyone."

With the Father and the Ruler at Abigail's side, the warriors stayed clear of her. But they closed around Watson like a cloud of locusts.

Dozens more warriors worked on the hall's pillars. The prince shouted, "Cripple the most respected in the hall, and you will bring the whole structure down!"

The gossip, complaining, faultfinding, and judgmentalism that had been growing now burst into the open as the factions each identified the people they believed to be a threat to the hall.

Then, it happened. The pillars down the center of the hall gave way, splitting the hall open from north to south. The great, wooden beams across the ceiling broke loose and fell, sending all the humans scurrying to the east and west sides of the hall. The Ruler, who stood with the Father on the west side, called out, "Come to me, all of you, and you will be safe."

All who loved the Ruler came to him. But the factious and those who had not forgiven Abigail could not see the Father or the Ruler. They had so convinced themselves that the Father couldn't possibly be with Abigail, they ran to the east side, expecting to find him there.

*****

The moment the pillars gave way, time froze for Watson. There was time to dash to safety on the west side. But the group he had just confronted were turning toward the east.

His sister's screams reached his ears. "Watson! *Run!*"

He looked at her and mouthed words he knew she would understand. Then he grabbed the sleeves of two men, pleading with them. "Come with me!"

Just as they shook him off, the massive timbers came down in a deafening crash.

Watson saw the beam a split-second before it hit him. Not enough time to even throw up his arms, much less to dive out of the way. In the blinding pain, he knew immediately his back was broken. Unable to move, he could only watch the second beam plummeting down upon him.

But this one he didn't feel. Was it adrenaline? Shock? In a surge of strength, he rose to his feet. Throughout the hall he saw people he didn't recognize. Some were angry and looked dangerous. Others friendly. All were armed and were engaged in combat.

Several of the friendly ones surrounded Watson, protecting him. They escorted him to the Ruler, who now shone with colors far more intense than any Watson had ever experienced. The moment Watson saw him, he felt himself change. The spectacular colors now emanated from his own body.

All pockets of confusion in his mind left him. Mysteries became clear. Joy coursed through his veins. Anxiety, fear, worry, boredom—none of them even seemed possible now. He could hardly remember what they felt like.

The Ruler held a huge cup with blue liquid running down the sides and offered it to Watson.

"For me? To … *drink*?"

The Ruler smiled.

Watson studied the cup. The idea of ingesting the fluid seemed … irreverent. He raised the cup to his mouth, keeping his eyes on the Ruler.

The Ruler nodded permission, and Watson tipped the fluid against his mouth, parted his lips, and sipped.

Power permeated his chest, then his stomach. Aches throughout his body—aches he never knew he had—made themselves known as they dissolved into pleasure. Life swelled within him and rose from his pores as if it were too much for his body to contain. Strength, energy, motivation, the ability to enjoy his surroundings—each component of life grew by the moment.

Watson lifted the cup to his mouth again, slowly, giving the Ruler another questioning look.

The Ruler reached and took the cup from his hand. He glanced inside the cup, then with a flip of his wrist, flung the remaining fluid to the ground.

"Follow me," he said, and led him out of the hall and down a trail Watson had never seen before.

The trees lining the path flourished with a much brighter, deeper green than normal. And every sight resolved in such sharp focus that Watson took pleasure in merely viewing all that stood before him—a pebble, a pine needle, and especially, the cottage directly ahead.

He put a hand to his eye. No patch—both eyes bright and clear.

The path opened into an expansive valley. A river filled the bottom—a river so wide he could hardly see the other side. But instead of water, it raged with a torrent of the blue liquid.

The Ruler handed Watson the empty cup. "I call it my river of delights."

Watson ran to the shoreline with speed that startled him. He dipped the cup and drank it dry. Then another. Joy boiled into laughter, tears, and singing.

*****

When the dust cleared, a pile of rubble divided the two sides of the banquet hall. As the people slowly awakened from their shock, they took in the devastation, still paralyzed in disbelief.

Those nearest the Father escaped serious injury. Charles had been momentarily deafened by the crash, but as his hearing recovered, cries and moans surrounded him.

"Layth. Levi. Help me." The two men hurried to help Charles free a woman trapped under a beam.

"Lift!" Layth and Levi managed to hold it just long enough for Charles and another server to pull the woman free.

The portion of the roof that had fallen blocked access to the other side. Judging from the small number on the west side, most of the people had either been crushed in the center or had chosen to run away from Abigail instead of toward her.

"Where is Abigail?" Charles asked.

"She went with Kailyn and Adam to check on the others," said Levi. "They went out the west doors so they could circle around the outside."

Charles' eyebrows jumped. "Abigail went to the east side?"

"She'll be okay. Adam is with them. They just wanted to check on everyone over there."

"How about Watson?"

"Haven't seen him," Levi said.

Charles looked at Layth, who shook his head.

"He said something to Kailyn just before the collapse," said Levi. "But I couldn't make it out."

Two servers approached with a report. "Six with serious injuries on this side. They're being treated, and we think they'll all make it. Two are critical, though. We'll have to watch them closely."

"I'll come check on them as soon as I can," said Charles. "In the meantime, make sure you—"

"Here they come." Layth nodded toward the doors. "This doesn't look good."

Kailyn, Abigail, and Adam approached, shoulders slumped, tears cutting channels through their dust-caked faces.

Adam composed himself enough to speak. "It's a mess over there. Hundreds of injuries. We tried to help, but when they saw Abigail, none of them would have anything to do with us. They blame her for the collapse."

"Any fatalities?" Charles asked.

Abigail's tears turned to audible sobs, and for a moment, Adam couldn't speak. He cleared his throat, and voice shaking, said, "Watson …" More tears. He cleared his throat again to give himself a moment. Then he whispered, "He's gone."

Layth covered his face with both hands and turned away, taking two or three aimless steps. Kailyn and Abigail embraced with renewed sobs. Charles sat in a daze.

The sounds faded and the chaos around him blurred into slow motion. *I should tend to the injured. I can grieve later*. But he couldn't move.

Levi faced Kailyn. "What did he say?"

She raised her eyebrows.

"Just before the collapse, Watson said something to you. I couldn't hear. Do you know what he said?"

She lowered her head. "They aren't …" More sobs choked off her words. She took a breath and tried again. "He said, 'They aren't … ready.'"

Kailyn turned to Layth, who closed his eyes and gave a slow nod.

The friends waited for an explanation, but none came. Finally, Levi asked, "What does that mean?"

"When we were in the gorge, after Kailyn fell out, Watson started to panic," Layth said. "But then he remembered the promise room. I watched his terror melt into calm. Then he said, 'I'm ready.'"

"They told me about it after we were reunited," Kailyn said. "And Watson explained what he meant. He said he was speaking to the Ruler when he said that. He was ready to die and face Judgment Day. He knew his faith was real and all his evils forgiven."

Levi frowned. "So, today when he said, 'They aren't ready' …"

"He was talking about the people he had confronted about Abigail," Kailyn said. "*He* was ready to die, but those people were not. He could see that they weren't coming to the Father, and he gave his life trying to bring them."

"Why would he do that?" Levi asked. "What's the point of throwing away a good life to save a bad one?"

"Don't you remember the blood room?" Charles said. "Giving a good life to save bad ones is exactly what the Ruler did for us. And it's what he taught us to do for one another."

"What a way to go," Layth said with a grin.

"Just like the ruler," Charles added.

Levi squirmed. His quizzical expression contracted into a pained one.

"What's wrong?" Charles asked. "Do you disagree?"

"It's not that. It's just …" He threw up his arms. "Two minutes ago you were all weeping. Now you're smiling. Does Watson's death mean so little to you? How can you take it so lightly?"

Charles' smile broadened. "I assure you, the tears were real, and there will be many more to follow as we feel the sting of our loss. But we don't grieve like the lowlanders. When they lose a loved one, he's lost forever. For us, it's temporary—like sleep. The Ruler has said, 'Whoever wants to save his life will lose it, but whoever loses his life for me will save it.'"

Charles went on, "One of my favorite places in the promise room is the death bed. Above it are the Ruler's words. 'I am the resurrection and the life. He who believes in me will live, even though he dies. And whoever lives and believes in me will never die.' We will see Watson again."

Chapter 23

Charles' spirit lay as crushed as the banquet hall. He'd spent his life laboring to bring about unity and love among the people and had taught many times about the Father's forgiveness. He thought everyone understood that forgiveness came, not on the basis of what the offender deserved, but on the basis of the forgiveness they themselves had received from the Father. Seeing most of the people retreat from Abigail made him wonder if his life's work had been for nothing.

That night as he lay in bed, desperate for the escape only sleep could provide, relentless consciousness plagued him. His thoughts rioted in a cacophony of disjointed ideas and a tangle of despair, self-pity, anger, and grief. His brain couldn't complete a thought without a dissonant idea breaking in upon it. The harder he tried to think the situation through, the more scrambled his mind became.

He soaked his bed with sweat. His heart raced. *I can't breathe!*

The room's darkness thickened. Pressure on his chest threatened to squeeze his life from him. He tried to sit up but couldn't move. Images of angry faces from the hall flashed across his consciousness. People he had humbly served and loved. People he had comforted on their sick beds. People he thought were some of his closest friends. Now they hated him.

His whimpers turned to deep, heaving moans. He retched, then tried to cry out in pain but had no voice. Time slowed, each moment an eternity.

*****

Ten vile warriors darted back and forth across Charles' room, assailing him with blow after blow. The prince of darkness stationed himself at the door, eyeing the six guardians who stood expressionless against the far wall. *Why are they not fighting? Perhaps Charles' faith has finally broken, or he has hidden sin and the Father has given him over to me.*

Still, something didn't seem right. His hand remained on his bow and he never took his eyes off the six dangerous statues.

Straining against his paralysis, Charles lifted a hand. It rose an inch, then fell to the mattress like a rag. The movement didn't escape the prince's notice. *Was he trying to pr—?*

With blinding light and speed that startled even the prince, all six guardians exploded into action. The warriors, caught off guard, were quickly driven out.

The prince lifted his bow but did not engage. He could easily defeat six guardians, but … was the wind blowing? *Something* was happening and he did not want to be in the room if the Ruler were to appear. Should he flee while he still could? Or try to quickly finish the job with Charles first?

The guardians' actions made no sense. Normally they would try to encourage Charles, lift his spirit, remind him of specific pieces of furniture from the promise room. But they did none of that. They simply whispered, "Come now. He's calling."

The prince flew into action, knocking all six guardians away with a single sweep of his bow. In an instant, he was on top of Charles. At all cost, he must not let him out of that bed.

*****

Charles regained his breath. His pulse slowed, and the terror vanished. A voice in his head whispered, *It was just a passing panic attack. You're fine now. Just roll over and go to sleep.*

The soothing light of the midnight moon coaxed Charles to stay in bed. He rolled over. *I've got to get some rest. Things will be clearer in the morning.*

The wind gusted and Charles recalled a story of the Ruler. "Very early in the morning, while it was still dark, the Ruler got up, left the house, and went to a secluded place where he prayed."

"He *is* calling me." Charles pushed into a sitting position.

This time the voice was louder. *Yes, he is calling you. You need to go meet with the Ruler. But not now. Wait until morning. If you try to talk to him now, you'll never be able to focus. Get some sleep and meet with him in the morn—*

A second gust roared through the room, raising another memory from the story of the Ruler. "During the days of his weakness, he offered up prayers and petitions with loud cries and tears to the one who could save him from death, and he was heard because of his reverent submission. Let us then approach the throne of the Father's favor with confidence, so we may receive mercy and find life from the Father to help us in our time of need."

It won't work, Charles, the voice insisted. *If he were going to give you the fluid, he would have done it by now. He entrusted you with oversight of the hall, and you made a mess of it. What you are feeling is just the natural consequence of your failure.*

*****

But the prince's frantic effort came too late. Charles' heart had already drunk in the Ruler's words like a flower in the sunlight. Hope sparked.

But the prince refused to give up. If he couldn't snatch the words away, he would choke them out with worry. *You need to figure out what you're going to do about the collapsed hall. What is your plan? And how are you going to deal with that while you have so many loose ends in your own life? Your roof has a leak. The grass in your yard is dying. You're not even close to living within your budget. You need to put your house on the market, or find a second job ...*

From deep within Charles came another gust of cottage words, so vivid in his thoughts, the prince could hear them. And they grated on his ears.

"Do not be anxious about anything, but in everything, by prayer and petition, present your requests to the Father, and his peace, which transcends understanding, will guard your heart and mind through your friendship with the Ruler."

Now Charles was speaking the words out loud. "As the deer pants for streams of water, so my soul pants for the Ruler. My body longs for him in a dry and weary land where there is no water. When can I go and meet with him? Why are you downcast, O my soul, why so disturbed within me? Put your hope in the Father, for I will yet trust him, my Savior and my God."

The wind must *be blowing!* The prince's eyes darted in every direction. Was the Ruler coming? Torturous memories of the last encounter with the Ruler melted his bones.

He fled from the house as fast as he could move.

*****

Charles rubbed his eyes. His body groaned with fatigue and pleaded with him to lie back down. "No," he whispered, then stumbled his way to the closet. He pulled on some clothes, descended the stairs, and pushed the front door open. The cold of the night greeted him, but he didn't go back for a jacket. He had been summoned, and he was going. Nothing else mattered.

He broke into a full sprint. Every moment delaying his arrival felt intolerable.

Darkness seemed to pursue him. He ran harder, but it overtook him. *What am I doing? It's the middle of the night. Will the Ruler even be there?* He slowed to a walk. He imagined arriving at the cottage only to find it locked. Empty. As vacuous as his own soul. *I have doubted the Ruler. Will I be shut out?*

He stopped. Sleepiness engulfed him. He turned. His home was still visible in the moonlight. His warm bed beckoned him. *Maybe I should wait until morning.*

He started toward home, but a stiff breeze kicked up, slowing his progress. He fought it, but it only intensified in a swirl of dust. He acquiesced and turned again toward the cottage.

The front of the cottage stood completely dark, but he saw lights inside. Before his hand reached the latch, the front door opened.

Charles fell to his knees in awe of the glorious splendor of the Ruler, who filled the doorway.

Charles lifted his eyes. "Did … you call me?" He already knew the answer but wanted to hear it from the Ruler himself.

"I did. And you did well to come. I want to show you the map room."

Charles hadn't expected that. Nor was it what he wanted. Normally, he would be thrilled to be shown the map room. He loved seeing the big picture of the Father's plans. But right now his mind refused to consider anything beyond the present crisis. A man doesn't care to plan his retirement at the moment he is bleeding out.

As they passed by the mirror room, Charles heard moans. A smile took over his face when he peeked in and saw the man who was in the throes of conviction, about to die and be reborn. It was Doctor Jensen.

Chapter 24

Charles entered the map room and was greeted by the smiling faces of Layth, Kailyn, Levi, Adam, Abigail, and several others who had run toward Abigail at the collapse.

Maps lined the walls. The first, to the right of the door, showed the garden that had surrounded the cottage when it was first built. Each successive map showed the progressive expansion from the garden throughout the high country as it stood now, including the most recent annex.

At the center of the room sat a large table with a new map, rolled up. Layth was the first to step forward. The others soon followed and crowded the table for a glimpse.

The Ruler waved for Charles to approach, and the group parted to let him near the table. "I want to show you my purposes in the recent events."

“You mean the freeing of Abigail?” Charles asked.

“I mean all of it.”

“But not the collapse of the hall,” Levi said. “Tell me you weren’t involved in that.”

“*All* of it,” the Ruler repeated as he unrolled the map.

Levi stepped closer and studied the map. “Okay. So what are all these lines? Looks like a starburst.” He pointed to an array of vectors all originating from the same point—a gleaming new banquet hall that stood on the site of the collapsed hall.

Charles’ heart ached over the demise of the hall entrusted to him but was glad to see that at least his failure would not hinder the progress of the great city. *Hopefully the new hall will fare better than mine.*

“The lines show the paths each of you will take on your next assignment,” the Ruler said. He traced a line with his finger. “This one is you, Levi.” He touched each of three other parallel lines. “Kailyn … Abigail … Adam. The four of you will go together when you’re ready.”

Abigail beamed, warming the whole room.

And Adam’s smile almost riveled hers. “When do we go?”

“That’s up to Charles,” said the Ruler. “You’ll be training under him. When he says you’re ready, that’s when you go.”

Charles stammered in disbelief. “Under … me? You will still … use me in the new hall? I … I thought

…" Sobs choked off his words as the anguish of his failure comingled with gratitude for a second chance.

"Yes, I will still use you," said the Ruler. "And no, it is not a new hall."

"But … this one is far greater than mine was, and"—he put his finger on the map—"it sits on the very spot of the wreckage."

The Ruler explained. "Your hall was not wrecked. It was cleansed. There must be factions to show who has my approval and who does not. If the unfaithful are never exposed, they only continue to tarnish the glory of the hall, even poisoning the food. For the hall under your care to reach its full glory, the contaminations had to be removed. What looks to you like a pile of rubble is, in my eyes, most glorious, because it is now pure."

The Ruler smiled at Charles. "And it was through your faithful labor—all the meals you served over the years—that I created that glory." He laid a hand on the weary server and squeezed his shoulder. "Well done, Charles!"

The words quelled Charles' anxieties like a mountain stream flowing over hot embers. Every fear melted into peace. Loss became gain. What none of Charles' efforts at self-comfort could even begin to achieve, the Ruler accomplished in just two words. Tears washed his face. Hope and joy pervaded his being. He knew there would still be heartaches, as always, but felt he could endure anything after those amazing words—*Well done!*

The Ruler unrolled the rest of the map. Gasps filled the room at where he had drawn the high-country's future eastern boundary. The river would flow along the very edge of the orchard.

The orchard itself, however, appeared much darker than before.

"In the last days," the Ruler explained, "the orchard will go from bad to worse. Appetites will become more and more perverse. At the same time, the high-country will gain more and more ground. The halls built with wood will be purified and become more glorious, while others—those mimicking the architecture in the golden city—adapt to the east and lose their glory."

"How long will all that take?" Kailyn asked. "The last time Layth and I were here you showed us a clock that had only days left before the judgment."

"The clock you saw was Abigail's, not the world's. Time was running out for her. Had you not gone when you did, she would have been lost forever. But we have not revealed the timing of the world's judgment. It could be near, but you must be prepared for a long delay as well."

Most intriguing to Charles were the four vectors that showed his friends' next assignment. They pointed to a new banquet hall that sat square on the orchard's border. "How could a banquet hall survive that close to the orchard?"

"It will be difficult," the Ruler replied, "requiring some specialized tools. For one thing, it will take great faith. The effort will have to be led by someone with unbounded energy. Someone who has recently come from the orchard so he can relate to people escaping. And above all, someone who trusts me to do the impossible."

Levi's eyes were circles as he gazed at the map. Then he looked up to discover all other eyes in the room trained on him.

"What?"

Laughter broke out.

"Seriously, Levi?" said Kailyn. "You're the only one in the room that doesn't realize he's talking about you?" She gave him a playful bump with her shoulder. "Come on *Abraham*—keep up."

Levi touched the bar with his new name. "How did you …"

Kailyn smiled, "It wasn't hard to guess. Abraham—the father of faith? I knew your new name as soon as I saw your weapon."

The Ruler winked at Levi. "What did I tell you? When I make a new creation, my people can see it."

He turned to the group. "To fill the hall, there will have to be a continual stream of new people coming in from the orchard. That will require someone"—he looked directly at Kailyn—"who is not afraid to do whatever it takes to persuade people from the orchard to come to me."

Kailyn bowed. "I will become anything to anyone—whatever it takes."

The Ruler turned from Kailyn and took Abigail's hand. "No one in this room loves me like Abigail. She who has been forgiven much loves much. I will plant her at the center of the new hall, and her love for me will diffuse throughout the hall like a sweet-smelling fragrance, permeating the hearts of the people, and stimulating joy. Through her smile I will make this the greatest of the banquet halls."

Remembering the hopeless case she had been just days earlier, Charles' heart swelled with happiness over his restored sister being so honored. Without thinking, he began to clap.

The others joined in. The applause grew with cheers and whistles as joy stoked joy in compounding celebration.

Levi nudged Charles. "Guess that means it will be even greater than your hall."

Charles winked at Abigail. "The greater, the better."

The Ruler turned to Adam. "The lead server of this hall must be a man with a profound appetite. He must crave my delicacies, but also know what it's like to be unable to taste real food so he can understand those who come with divided hearts. Beyond that, he must be able to unfold mysteries from the cottage that both stimulate and satisfy good appetites. And finally, the man who leads this hall must be one who celebrates every rescued soul, no matter how deformed."

He laid his hand on Adam. "I have taught you how to love not just the beautiful, but the broken."

Until this moment, the thought of being a server in a banquet hall had never crossed Adam's mind. But now he knew this was his destiny. The Ruler held the life of every creature in his hand, and whatever he drew on the maps was as certain as anything could ever be.

"Is this the meaning of my new name?" Adam ran his finger over the inscription on his chain—*David*.

"Yes. The name Adam means 'man.' When you first emerged from the pond, that was all you were. But my purpose in bringing you forth was to make you not just a man, but a man after my own heart. I created you to be a shepherd for my flock and to lead them to green pastures."

"What about before the pond?" he asked. "Why can't I remember my childhood?"

"Your existence began in the pond. The feelings that seem to you like memories are not memories. They are the imprint I placed on your soul of the home and family of your future."

"Are you saying I don't really have a family?"

The Ruler lifted his arm to the rest of the group. "This is your family! Abigail, Kailyn, Layth, Levi, and many, many more—sisters, brothers, mothers, fathers, sons, daughters. You will be rich beyond imagination in family love."

Abigail leaned in to Adam and he held her.

The Ruler smiled. "And *this* sister—you desire her as more than a sister?"

Adam gazed deeply into Abigail's eyes and took both her hands in his. "I do."

Abigail turned hopeful eyes to the Ruler like a child whose pleading face melts her father's heart.

The Ruler addressed Adam with a look that made him straighten like a soldier at attention. "You proved your love as a brother when her beauty was hidden. Now her full beauty will be unveiled to you and you may serve me together as one flesh."

The embrace that followed lit every heart in the room with joy.

Levi nudged Kailyn. "Do you think she even knows her feet aren't touching the ground?"

Kailyn smiled. "I promise you—she's not thinking about her feet right now."

Adam set Abigail down and turned to the Ruler. "This time I will be for her what I failed to be last time—a man who loves you first. After that, I will love her the way you loved us in the blood room."

He faced Abigail and drank in her renewed beauty.

The Ruler spoke again. "Abigail, honor me by honoring Adam. At his side, you will have power—more power than you'll ever know. Power to fortify him or weaken him. You must be a strengthening lifeline, a conduit of my enablement. It's the only way he will overcome the fierce opposition he will face."

Adam gently brushed a curl from Abigail's eyes. "How do you feel about working in a hall right at the orchard's border?"

"The only place I ever want to be is wherever the Ruler sends me."

"What's that—east of the city?" Layth said, pointing to the map. The Ruler had not unrolled the full map. Layth pushed the curled paper out, revealing the eastern section.

His eyes widened, and he stepped back. The others stood in stunned silence.

"It's impossible," Adam whispered.

That remark got him an elbow in the ribs from Levi. "You're seriously going to use that word when he's standing right here?" he said, shifting his eyes to the Ruler. "But seriously, who are you going to send for *that* operation?"

A loud moan echoed from the mirror room, and the Ruler smiled.

"The little guy?" Levi said. "No way!"

"That's a story for another day," The Ruler said as he rolled that portion of the map back up. "The doctor has much growing to do first, but yes, he will be the one."

All eyes fixed again on the Ruler. His confident smile set every anxiety at ease and filled each of the friends with courage. Faith, hope, and love were palpable in the room, and looking through the eyes of faith, each relished their assignment.

One by one, the friends migrated from the table to the final map at the end of the wall—everyone's favorite. On that map, no trace of the orchard remained. The glorious city covered the world and shone with colors even brighter than those of the cottage. Those colors, once unveiled, would never be hidden.

"It will happen," the Ruler assured them. "And each of you will rule that city with me forever."

He put his hand on Adam's shoulder. "From the day you rose out of the pond, you have been searching for freedom. But you've never known what freedom is." He pointed to the map. "*That* is freedom."

Adam squinted at the drawing then looked back to the Ruler.

"To pursue freedom, you must understand what enslaves you," said the Ruler. "Bondage is anything that puts a ball and chain on your ability to be what I created you to be. I made you to rule over the creation. But as long as your Judas desires remain, you will find yourself ruled by the creation. In the new world, I will set you free from all Judas desires. On that day, every shackle will be loosed and you will run like you've never run."

The Ruler stepped back, folded his arms, and gazed at the final map, his face painted with pure pleasure.

Then he took the new map from the table and tacked it up in its place on the wall.

He looked again at the final map. "Walk with the wind and grow in the Father's love and you will hasten that day."

"But for now,"—he went to the door and motioned for everyone to follow—"come, let's eat."

Dear Reader,

Thanks for reading! I pray you were edified by the story. If so, would you consider taking a quick moment to go to wherever you purchased this book and leave a review? A sentence or two is fine. It really helps others find the book.

For a chapter-by-chapter interpretation of the allegory, keep reading.

THE MEANING OF THE ALLEGORY

Chapter 1 Meanings

The Prince and the Creation

The prince of darkness (representing Satan) has the power to cause a flash flood. This illustrates the power God grants Satan to manipulate elements of the creation, as seen in Job 1:16-20, where Satan sends fire from the sky and a deadly desert wind.

Chapter 2 Meanings

Adam's Perception of the Cottage

After going through the blood room and promise room (symbolizing his conversion—coming to faith in Christ), Adam was a new man (illustration 2 Corinthians 5:17). What had appeared before as ordinary features of the building now shone with brilliance that surpassed anything in the golden city. This is to show the spiritual vision that comes when a person is born again, replacing his former blindness (see 2 Corinthians 4:4 and 1 John 2:11).

Adam's Gift

A hurricane, referred to as "he" (the Holy Spirit), gives Adam a gift. Adam expects to be pinned to the wall, but the power of the wind held him up and stabilized him. This shows that the awesome power of the Spirit, deadly when opposed, is for us when we come to him in faith.

Adam's gift is a pair of glasses that enable him to see seams in cottage pieces and unfold them, revealing more thorough understanding. The fact that cottage pieces have been folded a thousand times illustrates the truth that great volumes of truth are packed into each passage of Scripture, waiting to be unfolded by those who study it.

“The unfolding of your words gives light; it gives understanding to the simple” (Psalms 119:130).

“Reflect on what I am saying, for the Lord will give you insight into all this” (2 Timothy 2:7).

Adam’s glasses stand for the gift of knowledge—the unique ability to extract insights from God’s Word. The fact that Adam still has to study a long time to see the seams illustrates the hard work required even when a person has the gift of knowledge.

When Adam uses the glasses, he sees brilliant colors (God’s glory) and the wind swirls around him, causing his skin to drip with blue fluid (grace). This illustrates how the power of the Spirit is unleashed when we use our spiritual gifts, resulting in the dispensing of grace (1 Peter 4:10).

Adam is to place food into the mouths of the Father’s people by unfolding the cottage pieces for them. This illustrates the gift of teaching. Teachers are to feed God’s people with the Scriptures (John 21:15-17).

Sol’s Protection of Watson

Watson’s guardian was instructed to keep Watson alive, but not to interfere with the test. This shows that even when we are being protected by God, suffering can be intense. God protects our hearts, even as our bodies are ravaged. This illustrates passages like Luke 21:16-18, which promises not a hair on our heads will be harmed even as we are being put to death.

Chapter 3 Meanings

Watson's Failure

When Watson eats the berries (sin), he and Kailyn take it somewhat lightly ("live and learn, right?"). This illustrates inadequate, half-hearted repentance.

The stranger encourages this attitude, and pushes it further, popping berries into his mouth without shame. Watson and Kailyn feel freedom to follow his lead. This illustrates those who, in the name of fighting legalism, turn grace into a license for immorality (Jude 1:4).

Watson and Kailyn were being soundly defeated in the battle until Layth arrived and gently rebuked them. This is to show the importance of believers helping fellow believers who are straying.

"My brothers, if one of you should wander from the truth and someone should bring him back, remember this: Whoever turns a sinner from the error of his way will save him from death and cover over a multitude of sins" (James 5:19-20).

"Brothers, if someone is caught in a sin, you who are spiritual should restore him gently. But watch yourself, or you also may be tempted" (Galatians 6:1).

Layth's warning, "Live by Judas desires and you'll die!" comes from Romans 8:13.

"For if you live according to the flesh you will die, but if by the Spirit you put to death the deeds of the body, you will live" (Romans 8:13 ESV).

Layth's warning, "If any man says, 'I will be safe, even though I persist in going my own way'—the Father will never be willing to forgive him" is taken from Deuteronomy 29:19-20.

"When such a person hears the words of this oath, he invokes a blessing on himself and therefore thinks, 'I will be safe, even though I persist in going my own way.' … The LORD will never be willing to forgive him" (Deuteronomy 29:19-20).

Satan hates it when we help one another this way, so he works to prevent it—often by misusing Scripture, as he did when tempting Jesus in Matthew 4:6. In Watson's case, the evil spirit says, "*Why do you think you could help Abigail escape? You can't even resist a couple berries. Get the log out of your own eye before you try to help someone else.*"

This shows a combination of satanic strategies. First, self-deprecation. Satan works to bring us to a point of being so down on ourselves that we feel unfit to help others (as if the power to help others came *from* us, rather than *through* us).

The tactic works on Watson, causing him to drop his defenses. Satan uses self-condemnation to make us lower our defenses because he knows he can't defeat us unless we agree to join him in his accusing work and defeat ourselves. This is why we must listen to

God, not ourselves, when our hearts condemn us (1 John 3:20).

The evil spirit also appeals to Matthew 7:1-4, which speaks of removing the log from one's own eye before trying to remove the splinter in someone else's eye. This is a misuse of what Jesus said. Jesus' point was not that we must be sinless before we help others out of sin. The log doesn't represent sin; it represents *unrepentant* sin. We remove the log by repenting. It is not hypocritical to sin, repent, and then call on others to follow our example of repentance.

Layth urges Watson, "Resist, and he will flee!" When Watson asks how, Layth says, "Wash your hands. Purify your heart. Grieve, mourn, and wail. Change your laughter to mourning and your joy to gloom. Humble yourself. Return to the Ruler, and he will return to you." This is taken from James 4:7-10. The context is clear that resisting Satan so that he will flee is done through repentance.

"Submit yourselves, then, to God. Resist the devil, and he will flee from you. Come near to God and he will come near to you. Wash your hands, you sinners, and purify your hearts, you double-minded. Grieve, mourn and wail. Change your laughter to mourning and your joy to gloom. Humble yourselves before the Lord, and he will lift you up" (James 4:7-10).

Layth is fearless in facing Michael because, despite the prince's superior power, the one who sent Layth was far greater (illustrating 1 John 4:4).

When Watson does resist, the spirits flee in terror. (The word for "flee" in James 4:7 refers to running in fear.) In the story, the spirit's fear comes not from Watson's effort, but from the sudden appearance of the Ruler. The reason Satan flees in fear when we resist is that the power of our resistance comes from the Lord.

Layth explains that Watson's failure was egregious, not because he merely broke a rule, but because his action was an act of unfaithfulness to God. It is this relational way of looking at sin that shows why seemingly small sins are more serious than we naturally think. This is why Scripture compares sin against God to marital unfaithfulness (see, for example, James 4:4).

Layth goes on to explain that the Ruler "didn't take those wounds just to *pay* for your evils. He also suffered to *prevent* them. That's how much he desires your purity and eagerness to do good." This comes from Titus 2:14.

"Who gave himself for us to redeem us from all wickedness and to purify for himself a people that are his very own, eager to do what is good" (Titus 2:14).

When Watson resolves to confess his failure to the Father after the journey, Layth objects. "From the moment you eat fruit until you go before the Father, you allow the evil one to hold a place inside you." This illustrates Ephesians 4:27, which urges us not to give the devil a place.

The evil spirit counters by saying, "The Father is angry. Now is not the time to go seeking forgiveness. Give it some time. Let things cool off. He's not going to want to see you right now." This expresses the false idea that one should run from God when he is displeased. Scripture teaches that the only refuge from God's displeasure is his love. We must run toward him, not away from him when we sin (Zechariah 1:3).

The evil spirit goes on. "The Father will forgive you in time, but wait for his wrath to subside. For now, do some things you know are pleasing to him. Curry some favor. … But don't go asking for his favor now—it's too soon."

When we sin, Satan would have us believe we must earn God's favor. If that were possible, the cross would not have been necessary. All favor we receive from God, including forgiveness, comes not through our working for it, but by grace alone.

When Watson finally strikes back with his dagger, it is inscribed with, "Today, if you hear his voice, do not harden your heart" and "Seek the Lord while he may be found." These inscriptions are taken from Hebrews 3:15 and Isaiah 55:6.

Chapter 4 Meanings

The Ruler's Forgiveness

The moment Watson decides to return to the Ruler, the Ruler appears and rescues him. This illustrates Zechariah 1:3.

"…'Return to me,' declares the LORD Almighty, 'and I will return to you,' says the LORD Almighty" (Zechariah 1:3).

The Truth About the "Fruit"

The Ruler shows the friends the true nature of what they thought was fruit. In reality, it was maggots, scorpions, and sharp burrs. This is to illustrate the true nature of sin, which looks appealing on the outside, but once ingested turns bitter (Proverbs 5:3-4).

Keeping Charles Distracted

The evil spirits prevent Charles from coming to help the friends using a sickness in his family, unexpected home repairs, some financial problems, and a legal issue at the banquet hall. This is to illustrate how Satan uses the common worries of this life to defeat us (Mark 4:19).

Signs of Wind

The evil spirits are unable to detect the wind (the Holy Spirit), but they can watch for signs that he is at work, signs like joy, peace, self-control, and love. This is to illustrate that those virtues are the fruit of the Holy Spirit (Galatians 5:22-23).

Chapter 5 Meanings

Disharmony among the Friends

When the friends arrive at the orchard and begin the rescue effort, they are attacked by the enemy. But the attack comes in such an ordinary, mundane form that the friends don't see it as an attack. Irritability, selfishness, discomfort, self-pity, self-justification, and pride cause disharmony among the friends and threaten to derail the whole effort.

People often think of satanic attacks in terms of hardships in life. But Satan attacks us with temptation to sin, which can come through hardships or through pleasures. Satan can push us into pride or selfishness when times are pleasant or when they are difficult. It is not hardship that is our enemy, but sinful attitudes.

The attack is described in the story in two ways. First, from the human point of view (ordinary selfishness and irritability). Then from the spiritual point of view (in a heated conflict with evil spirits). This is to show that spiritual warfare can rage the hottest in some of the most mundane, normal moments in life.

Layth's javelin clanks to the ground in the moment when he is too lazy to use his gift and speak words of encouragement to Kailyn. This is to show that we are stewards in charge of dispensing God's grace (1 Peter 4:10). If we fail to do so, then brothers and sisters in Christ may be deprived of the grace they need.

Chapter 6 Meanings

Victory through Humility

The wind rescues Kailyn from this attack through conviction and by reminding her of the beauty of humility, patience, and love. His words, "Blessed are the meek. Be patient, tenderhearted, bearing with others in love" come from Matthew 5:5 and Ephesians 4:2.

It is when Kailyn humbles herself and asks forgiveness that the men are also humbled and confess. This derails all the work of the evil spirits and results in a decisive victory for the friends.

Strength through Obedience

After winning that battle, the spirits try to tempt the friends with all kinds of sins and the friends easily resist. This is to illustrate the truth of Galatians 5:16. When we keep in step with the Holy Spirit in one area, he gives us strength to defeat the flesh in other areas.

Seeking a Lost Sheep

Charles' words, "What kind of shepherd doesn't go after a lost sheep?" derive from Ezekiel 34:4, where the spiritual leaders of Israel are condemned for failing to go after those who have strayed.

Charles finally decided to go when he realized Abigail's eternal life was at stake. This illustrates James 5:20.

"My brothers, if one of you should wander from the truth and someone should bring him back, remember this: Whoever turns a sinner from the error of his way will save him from death and cover over a multitude of sins" (James 5:19-20).

This Kind ...

The prince is angry with Adramelech for merely tempting the friends with various sins without attacking their faith. "This kind can be defeated only after their faith is weakened." Just as there are some demons that are especially difficult to defeat (Jesus said, "This kind can only come out through prayer"), so it is on the other side of the battle lines. Those who have strong faith are impossible for demons to defeat. This is why Satan attempts to destroy our shield of faith. Otherwise, all his burning arrows are extinguished (Ephesians 6:16).

Self-Harm

When Abigail can't cross the border with her friends, she claws at her face, drawing blood. This is to illustrate the self-destructive nature of sin.

"But whoever fails to find me harms himself; all who hate me love death" (Proverbs 8:36).

Hopelessness

Abigail says, "Now my heart is hopelessly enslaved to the fruit. I can't break free." If the enemy can convince us that we are unable to resist a temptation, we will fall. This is why God reminds us that we are *always* able to resist (Philippians 4:13). The friends assure Abigail that there is always a way out (1 Corinthians 10:13).

Layth encourages her to persevere with these words taken from Galatians 6:9 and Hebrews 12:3-5. "Do not become weary. At the proper time, you will have success if you do not give up. Consider him who endured such opposition, so you will not grow weary and lose heart. In your struggle, you have not yet resisted to the point of shedding your blood. And you have forgotten that you are his daughter."

Chapter 7 Meanings

Clearing a Perimeter

Charles has the insight to know that Abigail's weakness is due to a problem in her heart. But diagnosing such a problem can take time. In the meantime, they protect her by clearing a perimeter. They chop down all the fruit trees surrounding their camp. This is to illustrate the first step in escaping an enslaving sin. Discovering the various heart issues can take time, but one thing can be done immediately. Clear a perimeter by removing any unnecessary temptation. Adjusting one's life to remain as far from temptation as possible will give some breathing room while deep heart issues are being addressed.

Distancing oneself from temptation as much as possible is always a wise practice. We must not go near the door of temptation's house (Proverbs 5:8).

Given over to the Enemy

The prince appears before the Father and requests that Abigail be given over to him as Alexander was. This is to illustrate 1 Timothy 1:20.

"Among them are Hymenaeus and Alexander, whom I have handed over to Satan to be taught not to blaspheme" (1 Timothy 1:20).

Running with Alexander

When Abigail is running from the mob and has to choose between Layth or Alexander for protection, she goes to Alexander, because he is physically stronger. This is to illustrate the temptation to revert to the world's solution to our problems rather than spiritual solutions. See Psalm 1.

I Would Have Given You Even More

When Abigail is trapped underground, the wind speaks to her. "I gave you a loving family. I gave you greater joy than anyone in the high country. I gave you your beauty and your smile. I gave you life, and—" She expected the rest to be something like, "I gave you all those gifts, and this is the thanks I get? You ignore me and eat fruit?" Instead he says, "If that had been too little, I would have given you even more."

This is to illustrate God's words to David after his sin with Bathsheba.

" … I anointed you king over Israel, and I delivered you from the hand of Saul. I gave your master's house to you, and your master's wives into your arms. I gave you the house of Israel and Judah. And if all this had been too little, I would have given you even more. Why did you despise the word of the LORD by doing what is evil in his eyes?" (2 Samuel 12:7-9).

God will continue to give to us until our souls are satisfied if we don't derail the process by opting for a sinful alternative.

The wind goes on to tell her that only he can promise to satisfy her soul. This illustrates the truth of Isaiah 55:1-2, which calls the world's alternatives "not bread" (that is, they don't satisfy).

Abigail's favorite title for the Father is *He who gives generously to all without finding fault*. This is taken from James 1:5.

Chapter 8 Meanings

Adam's Inability to Taste

Adam discovers the reason he couldn't taste the food on his first visit to the banquet was due to a divided heart. He was there partly because of the Ruler and partly because of Abigail. This is to illustrate the requirement that one must follow Christ wholeheartedly or not at all. Christ must be so far ahead of all other loves that our love for others seems like hatred in comparison.

"If anyone comes to me and does not hate his father and mother, his wife and children, his brothers and sisters-- yes, even his own life—he cannot be my disciple" (Luke 14:26).

A New Heart

"Something strong pulsed within Adam's chest. Something … *new*."

This illustrates the new heart God creates in a person who is born again.

"I will give you a new heart and put a new spirit in you; I will remove from you your heart of stone and give you a heart of flesh" (Ezekiel 36:26).

Enslaving Desires

The plaque in the wisdom room that says, "The desires of the unfaithful imprison them" is taken from Titus 3:3, which speaks of being enslaved by passions and desires.

Turning toward God

Abigail is mystified as to why the wind was never at her back, no matter which direction she went. Adam explains it was because she was only trying to leave the orchard but wasn't concerned about returning to the Father. This is to illustrate that repentance is not merely turning from sin. It is turning from sin *to God*" (Acts 3:19).

Chapter 9 Meanings

I Won't Leave You

Adam promises, "No matter how many times you stumble, I won't leave you." This is to illustrate that there is no limit to how many times we must be willing to forgive a repentant sinner (Matthew 18:21-22).

He goes on to say, "My mission is to present you to the Ruler safe and sound." This is taken from Paul's example.

"I am jealous for you with a godly jealousy. I promised you to one husband, to Christ, so that I might present you as a pure virgin to him" (2 Corinthians 11:2).

The Happiness Room

Both Adam and Abigail found the happiness room empty at first. Adam finally found joy because he persisted in searching for the Ruler. This is to illustrate the necessity to seek hard after God.

"You will seek me and find me when you seek me with all your heart" (Jeremiah 29:13).

When Adam did finally find him, joy didn't come from merely seeing the colors. Happiness came when he touched them. This is to show that it is not enough to be educated about God's attributes. The joy of fellowship with God comes only when we have delightful experiences with those attributes. When Scripture speaks of knowing God, it is the experiential, relational knowledge (Genesis 4:1 uses the same word when it says Adam *knew* his wife Eve and she conceived.)

When Adam touched the colors, he gained more than happiness. He said the experience was better than life itself (see Psalms 63:3).

Abigail found joy rising within her as she "touched" two of the Father's colors (his love and wisdom). She experienced these through Adam, showing that God's attributes can be experienced through people. God often delivers his love through people (Acts 9:15).

"A river of joy rose within her, fed by the three tributaries of gratitude from past experiences with the Ruler, hope of future encounters, and delight in her enjoyment of his colors in the present."

When all three "tributaries" of joy flow (from past, present, and future enjoyment of God), even the most stubborn Judas desires will give way to good desires.

Future enjoyment of God comes through hope. Adam's promise that the Father's colors are new every morning comes from Lamentations 3:23.

Chapter 10 Meanings

Empowering Grace

When Adam rubs the blue fluid (grace) on his arms, he can wield the heavy sword with superhuman power. This illustrates the enabling, strengthening effect of grace, especially in the use of the sword (Scripture). See 1 Corinthians 15:10 and Hebrews 13:9.

Don't Look

Adam advises Abigail not to look at the fruit as they make their way through the orchard. This is because temptation is activated in powerful ways through the eye gate (Genesis 3:6, 1 John 2:16).

Chapter 11 Meanings

The "Off" Button

Adam explains how Abigail can turn evil desires off through gratitude. This section expounds on the principle in Ephesians 5:3-4, where the solution to sins of greed, such as sexual immorality, impurity, or covetousness is thanksgiving. One cannot feel both gratitude and greed at the same time because greed focuses on what hasn't been given, while gratitude delights in what has been given.

Did It Fail?

When Watson is discouraged at the apparent failure of their mission, Charles points out that it was not a failure because the friends succeeded in carrying out the Father's will. This is a reminder that God's will has mainly to do with righteous attitudes and behavior, not gaining outward success in our endeavors (1 Thessalonians 4:3).

Chapter 12 Meanings

The *Stay Alert* book

The friends utilize the prince's strategy manual, which reveals all his tactics. The use of this book is to illustrate what it means to be aware of the devil's schemes (2 Corinthians 2:11). It's called the "Stay Alert" book because knowledge of Satan's schemes is part of the alertness required to avoid being devoured by Satan (1 Peter 5:8) as we take our stand against his schemes (Ephesians 6:11).

The first scheme Abigail reads of is the way Satan pushes us into irritability when sinful alternatives to God's food and drink leave us unsatisfied. For an example, see Amnon's response when he tries to satisfy himself through rape in 2 Samuel 13:14-15.

The second satanic strategy Abigail discovers is rationalization—deceiving ourselves into thinking a sin is justified (like Saul in 1 Samuel 15). Rationalizing sin is self-deception (1 John 1:8).

The third satanic scheme is to convince us we are strong enough to handle temptation, so there is no need to avoid it. For an example of someone who fell for this scheme, see Proverbs 7:7-23.

The next tactic is self-pity. Feeling sorry for yourself makes gratitude impossible because it turns the focus from what God has given to what he has not given. The solution, as Abigail discovers, is gratitude to the Father for his gifts.

Next, evil curiosity. "Whisper to the subject, 'I wonder if this is a sweet one. I could take just a tiny, little taste. That wouldn't count as *eating* fruit.'" Jesus taught us to pray, "Lead us not into temptation." How can we pray that while we willingly run into the proximity of temptation?

Finally, using past failure to rationalize more failure. "I've already blown it now. I might as well just finish off the bunch and try to do better tomorrow." The folly of this is obvious. It's like saying, "I've fractured my leg, why not smash it to pieces?"

It is when the book alerts Abigail to these strategies that she spots the lion in time to escape. If we are alert to Satan's schemes that we can see them coming and flee before falling into sin.

Spiritual Armor

When Adam faces Alexander and the lion, he is victorious because he covers himself with armor. This is to illustrate the spiritual armor described in Ephesians 6:10-17.

One way the armor helps Adam is by making him sure-footed, so he doesn't slip or fall in the battle. This is to illustrate the "feet fitted with the readiness that comes from the gospel of peace" (Ephesians 6:15).

Adam's helmet and sword picture the helmet of salvation and the sword of the Spirit (Ephesians 6:17).

Adam shows Alexander that his freedom is imagined. In reality, he is a slave to his own stomach (see Philippians 3:19).

When Adam defeats Alexander, rather than celebrating, he is heartbroken out of compassion for Alexander. This mirrors the heart of Jesus, who wept when he pronounced judgment on those who were to crucify him (Luke 19:41).

Chapter 13 Meanings

The Vials

The friends explain to Abigail how they obtained whole vials full of the fluid (grace). "Every time your heart draws near to him to enjoy his colors, he adds to the vial." This illustrates what theologians call the means of grace—actions we can take to receive more grace from God. Chief among these is fellowship with God. As we draw near to him, we receive more of his favor (James 4:8).

Other means of grace include Scripture (Acts 20:32), prayer (Luke 11:13), and fellowship (Acts 2:42-47). Layth points this out to Abigail when he asks, "When is the last time you had a good meal?" She is weak because she has been deprived of the means of grace.

When Abigail has her first meal with the friends, eating feels like a chore. This is to illustrate how the avenues of drawing near to God, such as reading the Bible, prayer, and attending church, can feel burdensome to a person who is distant from God. Seeking God is not easy. When the wind tells Abigail she must be like the chicks with their mouths wide, fighting for the next bite, she learns of the importance of earnestness in seeking the Father (Jeremiah 29:13, Psalm 63:1).

Good and Bad Sorrow

Adam serves a meal in which he teaches about good and bad sorrow. This is taken from 2 Corinthians 7:10.

"Godly sorrow brings repentance that leads to salvation and leaves no regret, but worldly sorrow brings death" (2 Corinthians 7:10).

Adam reminds the group to preach to their soul (for an example of this, see Psalms 42 and 103). Talking to yourself about your sin results in self-condemnation and discouragement. Better to talk to God about your sin and to yourself about God.

The Catalyst

Charles explains that the fluid (grace) must be activated by a catalyst (trust). It is through faith that God's grace becomes active in our lives (Romans 4:16).

Chapter 14 Meanings

Assisted Fear

Abigail was not tempted with fruit while she was surrounded by her friends. Charles explains how her fear of eating fruit in front of disapproving friends assists her in fearing the Father. This is to illustrate how exposure and openness in the way we live can help us in our fight against sin. See 1 John 1:7-10 and Ephesians 5:8-15.

Self-Condemnation

When Abigail struggles with self-condemnation, Watson says, "Your heart is condemning you, not the Ruler. Which assessment matters—yours, or his?" This is to reflect the principle in 1 John 3:20, where the solution to self-condemnation is to remember that God is greater than our hearts. His judgment trumps our own.

Chapter 15 Meanings

Abigail's Favorite Piece

The chapter opens with Abigail holding a cottage piece that says, "Ask, and you will receive if you believe and don't doubt. The double-minded receive nothing. Persevere!" This is a combination of Matthew 7:7 and James 1:4-8.

Levi's Unwitting Assault

Levi arrives with the friends and makes a simple affirmation of trusting God, unknowingly dealing a devastating blow to the prince. This is to show the power that is unleashed through faith. Faith is the slender nerve that moves the mighty muscle of omnipotence.[1]"

---

[1] C. H. Spurgeon, from the sermon "The Ravens' Cry" delivered January 14, 1866.

Chapter 16 Meanings

Cleaning Yourself up

Michael draws attention to Abigail's disgusting appearance and suggests she make herself more presentable before appearing before the Father.

The ugliness of Abigail's appearance illustrates the way our hearts appear to God when there is unforgiven sin. Sin is consistently portrayed in Scripture in terms of all that is unclean, ugly, and disgusting. The great cry in the heart of the repentant sinner is to be cleansed in God's sight (Psalm 51:2).

Satan might attempt to prevent you from approaching God by pointing out your filthiness in God's sight. But the idea that we can clean ourselves or make ourselves presentable before God is to deny the gospel. If we could clean ourselves, the cross would not have been necessary. As Charles points out, we can no sooner cleanse our own sin than a leopard can change its spots (Jeremiah 13:23).

Charles goes on to say that trying to make yourself clean in the Father's sight only makes you more detestable in his sight. An example of this is the self-righteous Pharisee who depended on his own goodness and went away unjustified in God's sight (Luke 18:12-14).

The cottage saying, "I found you in your ugliness, kicking in your blood. Then I touched you and made you the most beautiful of jewels" is taken from Ezekiel 16:6-7.

Team Warfare

Each of the friends' gifts plays a role in winning the battle. Levi's faith boosts the faith of the others. Layth's encouragement protects the group from despair. Watson's wisdom keeps the others alert to the enemy's schemes. Kailyn's courage inspires Abigail. Charles' teaching keeps the group on track, and Adam's insight, leadership, and selfless love overcomes the enemy's advances.

This illustrates the need for all people to contribute to the overall effort of the church with their gifts (Ephesians 4:16, 1 Corinthians 12:12, Romans 12:4-8).

The Cloud of Privacy

As the group walks, the friends begin to stumble when the lowland cloud thickens. It was discovered this was due to hidden sin among them. Where sin goes unconfessed, darkness descends and the whole church is affected. This is illustrated by the sin of Achan in Joshua 7.

Charles vs. Charles

As the group sleeps, Charles does battle with his old self. This is to illustrate that our old self doesn't disappear when we are born again. It reappears constantly, temping us to behave like an unbeliever. For this reason, we must continuously "put off" our old self (Ephesians 4:22).

In Charles' case, his old self tempted him in the direction of man-pleasing. Charles' response, "If I'm driven by fear of people's opinion of me, I am no longer the Ruler's servant" is derived from Galatians 1:10.

Don't Give up!

Just as the prince is ordering his ranks not to give up, Charles exhorts the friends to persevere as well. This speech reflects the many passages in Scripture that call for perseverance.

"Let us not become weary in doing good, for at the proper time we will reap a harvest if we do not give up" (Galatians 6:9).

He calls it a "good fight" (1 Timothy 1:18) and says, "Your confidence will be richly rewarded if you don't throw it away. You need to persevere so that when you have done the Father's will, you will receive what he has promised." This comes from Hebrews 10:35-36.

Charles went on. "Say 'No!' to every evil thought within five seconds." Nancy Reagan was mocked for her "Just say no" campaign, but saying no is part of what God's grace teaches us to do.

"For the grace of God that brings salvation has appeared to all men. It teaches us to say "No" to ungodliness and worldly passions, and to live self-controlled, upright and godly lives in this present age" (Titus 2:11-12).

Charles goes on. "Say, 'No!' to every evil thought within five seconds. Give it more unopposed time than that and it will lodge itself and become almost immovable. Say it out loud. Be warlike and fierce" This is a paraphrase of the N point in John Piper's ANTHEM acronym for fighting lust.[2]

The final threat to the friends' perseverance at the end of the chapter is boredom. The monotony of the journey makes them crave stimuli, which makes them vulnerable to the birds (the world's entertainment) in the next chapter.

---

[2] https://www.desiringgod.org/articles/anthem-strategies-for-fighting-lust

STUDY GUIDE SAMPLE

Chapter 17 Meanings

The Birds

The cloud of birds fools the group into thinking it is the Father's colors (God's glory). But Adam shows them that isn't the case, because the cloud leads away from the Father instead of toward him. Our enjoyment of earthly pleasures should draw us nearer to God. When it becomes a substitute for God, we have crossed into idolatry. This is why any form of greed is idolatrous (Colossians 3:5).

Charles shows the group that the cloud is not the Father's colors because it lacks splendor, majesty, wisdom, mercy, and patience. "They amuse, but they don't fortify the soul." In other words, they turn out to be bread that is "not bread" (Isaiah 55:2).

Thought Control

As the friends enter the final battle, Charles reminds them to send each thought through a grid. "Is it true? Is it noble and right? Pure and lovely? Admirable? Excellent? Praiseworthy? If not, drive it out!" This reflects Philippians 4:8.

Layth vs. Anzu

In Layth's epic battle with the evil spirit Anzu, the story jumps between seeing the encounter from the human point of view (a mundane story about a guy who is tempted to forgo the hard work of trying to comfort a depressed friend), to the spiritual point of view (a violent battle against a powerful evil spirit).

This is another reminder that the battle is not against flesh and blood, but against spirits (Ephesians 6:12). Layth realizes a spirit is involved when it is unusually difficult for him to muster the energy to encourage his friend.

Abigail vs. Abigail

Just as Charles had to fight his old self, so does Abigail. This is the fight Adam had in mind when he spoke of the crisis Abigail would face ("When the time comes, will you strike?"). This battle represents the war between the Spirit and the flesh described in Galatians 5.

At one point in the fight, Abigail recalls the words, "My favor that brings salvation teaches you to say 'No' to old passions as you wait for me." This is taken from Titus 2:11-12. Her statement, "He died to purchase my purity" is also in that passage.

The image suggests Abigail might as well enjoy fruit, since the Father is so willing to always forgive.

Abigail counters by saying, “Destroy a relationship just because it’s possible to rebuild it? That’s like saying, ‘My leg can heal, so why not break it?’”

This is to highlight the fact that forgiveness is more than mere pardon or commutation of a penalty. It is the restoration of a broken relationship.

She also points out that a broken leg, while it can heal, can also lead to death. The same is true of a broken relationship with God (see James 5:20).

When Abigail is faced with the fact that she can never enjoy fruit again, she hesitates. At this point, she almost loses the battle. But then she remembers the words, “What benefit did you receive at that time from the things you are now ashamed of?” This is taken from Romans 6:21.

Chapter 18 Meanings

Stage Two

After what seemed to be a devastating loss to the evil spirits, the prince is ready to move on to the next stage in his plan, which is an attack on the banquet hall. The plan is to use Abigail's return to divide the hall by tempting many to withhold forgiveness and hold an attitude of superiority and self-righteousness.

This is to illustrate the need for churches to always forgive repentant sinners, and not to inflict further punishment on them. It is not the church's role to punish or teach the person a lesson. In fact, it is the church's responsibility to see to it that the person is not overcome with excessive sorrow (2 Corinthians 2:6-8).

Levi's Dead Body

When the group encounters Levi's dead body on the path, the new Levi is embarrassed. This represents the shame Christians often feel over the person they once were. The old self is depicted as a dead carcass in the story to reflect Romans 6:6, which says the old self was crucified.

River Reroute

The friends emerge from the forest to find the river has moved eastward, enlarging the high country territory. This represents the progress of the kingdom of God as it expands, pushing back the world's evil frontiers.

"Then Jesus asked, 'What is the kingdom of God like? What shall I compare it to? It is like a mustard seed, which a man took and planted in his garden. It grew and became a tree, and the birds of the air perched in its branches.' Again he asked, 'What shall I compare the kingdom of God to? It is like yeast that a woman took and mixed into a large amount of flour until it worked all through the dough" (Luke 13:18-21).

Biting and Devouring

News reaches Charles that the people in the banquet hall (church congregation) are biting and devouring one another.

"If you keep on biting and devouring each other, watch out or you will be destroyed by each other" (Galatians 5:15).

He also says the people are hardly eating. Those who come to the banquets but refrain from eating represent people who come to church but receive no grace from God. They go through the motions, but they are not seeking God.

Inside Job

Charles then learns that the wolves came from within the hall—from among the servers (pastors). This illustrates Paul's warning to the Ephesian elders.

"I know that after I leave, savage wolves will come in among you and will not spare the flock. Even from your own number men will arise and distort the truth in order to draw away disciples after them" (Acts 20:29-30).

Charles arrives to find the people divided into factions. This is typical in an unhealthy church.

"My brothers, some from Chloe's household have informed me that there are quarrels among you. What I mean is this: One of you says, 'I follow Paul'; another, 'I follow Apollos'; another, 'I follow Cephas'; still another, 'I follow Christ'" (1 Corinthians 1:11-12).

The Ruler's Delay

Charles' guardians wonder why the Ruler does not allow them to comfort Charles. The answer is that in order for Charles to digest the delightful meal the Ruler has for him, he must first be ravenously hungry.

This shows how we often need to be brought to desperation before we receive what the Lord has for us. An example is David in Psalm 63.

The guardians trust that "the pain the Ruler brought upon his people, while sharp, was never pointless."

"For our light and momentary troubles are achieving for us an eternal glory that far outweighs them all" (2 Corinthians 4:17).

Chapter 19 Meanings

Stunned by the condition of the hall, Layth, Kailyn, and Watson commiserate over tea. Layth reminds them, "The Ruler can be trusted—period. Trusting only when things make sense ain't trusting."

When people say they would trust God if they only knew why he allowed what he allowed, they show a faulty understanding of the concept of trusting. If we can see how something is good, trust isn't necessary. It is when we can't see that we need to trust the one who can. This is what it means to live by faith and not by sight (2 Corinthians 5:7).

Layth spoke "as a man trying to convince himself of his own words." This is like the man in Mark 9.

"… I do believe; help me overcome my unbelief!" (Mark 9:24).

Jensen's Stronghold

Levi finds a solitary spot, but is soon joined by Dr. Jensen, who has been sent by evil spirits to deceive Levi. His efforts to do so are portrayed as a spiritual stronghold rising around Levi and threatening to entrap him.

This illustrates the strongholds of 2 Corinthians 10:4. Some teach that a satanic stronghold is a geographical region where a particular sin is especially dominant. But that idea is not present in the context of 2 Corinthians 10. The passage speaks not of geographical regions or particular dominant sins, but rather of ideas.

"The weapons we fight with are not the weapons of the world. On the contrary, they have divine power to demolish strongholds. We demolish arguments and every pretension that sets itself up against the knowledge of God, and we take captive every thought to make it obedient to Christ" (2 Corinthians 10:4-5).

A satanic stronghold is any idea, concept, or argument that opposes the truth. And we demolish those strongholds by taking those ideas captive and forcing them into obedience to Christ. In other words, we preach the truth of the gospel and expose the error of wrong ideas.

When faced with the stronghold of self-esteem, Levite shouts to Levi, "Remember the mirror room!" The mirror room is the law of God, which acts as a mirror to expose the sin in our hearts. That room would remind Levi that the truth about himself was nothing to esteem highly. The solution is not higher self-esteem or self-anything. Rather, the goal is to esteem others more highly than oneself.

"Do nothing out of rivalry or conceit, but in humility consider others as more important than yourselves" (Philippians 2:3 CSB).

The friends demolish the self-esteem stronghold with the truth.

Watson says, "Loving the Father and others is only possible when we disregard the esteem we have for ourselves. To follow the Ruler, one must deny himself—not love himself" (see Luke 9:23).

Layth adds, "Do nothing out of selfish ambition or vain conceit, but in humility consider others more important than yourselves. Love is not self-seeking" (see Philippians 2:3 and 1 Corinthians 13:5).

Watson then says, "When we do evil, we must rend our hearts. We should grieve, mourn, and wail and change our laughter to mourning and our joy to gloom" (Joel 2:13 and James 4:9).

The Wind vs. Dr. Jensen

After their barrage of truth, Jensen feels a breeze, illustrating the work of the Holy Spirit on an unbeliever (see John 16:8). His feet begin to shrink, indicating a humbling of his heart.

Good Sorrow Bad Sorrow

The discussion that follows is about Abigail's agonizing sorrow. Levi simply wants to cheer her up, but Watson points out that the good kind of sorrow leads to repentance and life. They need only protect her from the bad kind of sorrow, which leads to self-destruction and death.

"Godly sorrow brings repentance that leads to salvation and leaves no regret, but worldly sorrow brings death" (2 Corinthians 7:10).

This truth is illustrated by contrasting Peter with Judas. Both committed the same sin in betraying Jesus. Both were sorrowful afterward. But Peter's sorrow led him to repentance, while Judas' sorrow led him to suicide (Matthew 27:3-5).

Colorlessness

Abigail hesitates to enter the hall because she feels colorless. Adam argues that the hall is the place where colors are infused. This illustrates those who use unworthiness as an excuse not to go to church. The church is the primary means God uses to solve the problem of sin in our lives (Ephesians 4:11-12). So being sinful is a reason to go, not a reason to stay away.

He argues further that it is through his people that the Ruler dispenses his love (1 John 4:12) and it is through loving others that one receives the most joy (John 15:11-12).

Finally, Adam says, "Even if there are wolves, if the Ruler is there, and it's where he serves his food, where else can you go?" This reflects Peter's words when Jesus asked if the disciples were going to leave him with the others.

“Simon Peter answered him, "Lord, to whom shall we go? You have the words of eternal life’” (John 6:68).

Chapter 20 Meanings

Unforgiveness

The response to Abigail's return is mixed. Some welcome her while others look down on her. Charles explains why. "'Those who remember their own bondage in the orchard will celebrate your return. Those who have forgotten their former bondage, or who imagined theirs to have been a bondage of lesser shame, will tolerate your presence. And those who are still in bondage but don't realize it will'—he motioned toward Hodia and the other woman—'do that.'"

This is to show the principle Jesus taught about forgiveness in the parable of the unforgiving servant (Matthew 18:23-35). A servant is forgiven an astronomical debt and then refuses to forgive a fellow servant a much smaller debt. The parable shows that if we are conscious of how much we have been forgiven, we will gladly forgive others. Those who refuse to forgive have either forgotten how much they have been forgiven or don't believe their sins required much forgiveness in the first place.

"Of course we all forgive her. But there are consequences for what she did."

"Are there consequences for other evils like, say, unforgiveness? Or self-righteousness? Or maybe pride? How about gossip?"

The server's face reddened. "That's not the same thing."

This exchange illustrates the attitude of many in the church who see themselves as better than those who commit scandalous sins, such as adultery or stealing. They see those sins as being in a worse class than their own more acceptable sins. But in Scripture, sins like slander and greed are placed right alongside sins like drunkenness and sexual immorality (1 Corinthians 5:11). And self-righteousness is a sign that a person isn't a believer.

"Two men went up to the temple to pray, one a Pharisee and the other a tax collector. The Pharisee stood up and prayed about himself: 'God, I thank you that I am not like other men—robbers, evildoers, adulterers—or even like this tax collector. I fast twice a week and give a tenth of all I get.' But the tax collector stood at a distance. He would not even look up to heaven, but beat his breast and said, 'God, have mercy on me, a sinner.' I tell you that this man, rather than the other, went home justified before God. For everyone who exalts himself will be humbled, and he who humbles himself will be exalted" (Luke 18:10-14).

Abigail is patient with the self-righteous, unforgiving people because she sees they are in bondage to their sin just as she was in bondage to her own. She didn't make the same mistake they were making, namely, considering her sin in a different class from theirs. The result was that instead of anger, she felt compassion for them.

"Be kind and compassionate to one another, forgiving each other, just as in Christ God forgave you" (Ephesians 4:32).

Man-Pleasing

Once again, Adam is tempted with the sin of man-pleasing. He wants to fit in with the people of the hall. But to do so, he must join in their gossip and self-righteous attitudes.

"He said to them, 'You are the ones who justify yourselves in the eyes of men, but God knows your hearts. What is highly valued among men is detestable in God's sight'" (Luke 16:15).

His guardian helps him resist this temptation by saying, "Mind your feet." Small feet represent pride. Wanting to be accepted and thought well of by others is a desire for earthly greatness. Jesus taught that those who have earthly greatness will be last in his kingdom, and the humble will be first (Mark 9:33-35).

Delayed Forgiveness

"We believe in restoration. In time, if she proves herself, she will be welcomed back."

This reflects the attitude some Christians have that before a repentant sinner can be fully restored to fellowship, there must be a time of proving that the repentance is genuine. But Scripture calls for forgiveness that is so immediate that a person can be forgiven, then sin again, be forgiven again, and so on seven times in a single day (Luke 17:4).

Siding with the Repentant

Adam is tempted to disassociate himself from Abigail to save face with the gossips. When the Apostle Paul was in Abigail's shoes, all the believers around him abandoned him. Only the Lord stood with him (2 Timothy 4:17-18). Adam shows his heart is with the Ruler's when he defies the crowd and defends Abigail.

Adam quotes the Father. "I live in a high and holy place, but also with him who is contrite and lowly in spirit, to revive the spirit of the lowly, and to revive the heart of the contrite." This is drawn from God's description of himself in Isaiah 57:15.

Stopping Their Ears

"The prince of darkness had both hands pressed firmly against the man's ears, so none of Adam's words penetrated. He had also hardened the others' hearts so thoroughly that Adam's words landed like seeds on a paved road."

This shows Satan's work of preventing unbelievers from receiving the truth of the gospel (see 2 Corinthians 4:4 and Mark 4:15).

Chapter 21 Meanings

The Sorrow of Repentance

When Abigail is overcome with grief over her sin, Watson affirms her sorrow.

"What Abigail is doing is beautiful. True repentance is a powerful internal force and it *will* come out. It must vent itself at the eyes by weeping, and at the mouth by confessing. Just as the body will expel poison from the stomach, confession does the same for the soul. That is why the Ruler instructs us to confess our sins to one another so that we may be healed."

This is a paraphrase of a passage from Thomas Watson's book, *The Doctrine of Repentance*. It was that book that inspired me to write the Walk with the Wind novels. They began as a short story designed to remind me of the truths I learned in Watson's book but then grew into a two-volume story. This is why the Watson character, who speaks these words, is named after Thomas Watson.

The following is another paraphrase from Watson's book:

"When a man's confession runs through him like water through a pipe, leaving no wounds on the heart, it remains superficial. Many declare resolutions to change when they are in the throes of bondage, but those vows dissolve once the hard consequences of evil are removed."

The Meal

The meal Charles served was a sermon on the prodigal son parable in Luke 15. His telling of the parable is intertwined with a dramatization of the parable where Abigail was the prodigal.

The main point of the prodigal son parable has to do with the older brother, who grumbled at the prodigal's return. This mirrors the grumbling of the Pharisees over Jesus welcoming repentant sinners—a response that prompted the parables in the chapter.

The older brother's grumbling ruins an otherwise wonderful moment in the story. This is to show how the Pharisees' grumbling about the sinners in Jesus' presence ruined an otherwise wonderful story of restoration and forgiveness.

This sets up the scene where everyone in the hall had to choose whether to side with Abigail or continue to reject her. Those who side with her, side with the Ruler and the Father. The others run the opposite direction and are shown to be rejected by the Father.

Washing Abigail's Feet

Before Abigail can appear before the Father, the Ruler must wash her feet. She objects, but he tells her he will not accompany her unless she allows him to wash her. This comes from the exchange between Jesus and Peter in the upper room.

"He came to Simon Peter, who said to him, 'Lord, are you going to wash my feet?' Jesus replied, 'You do not realize now what I am doing, but later you will understand.' 'No,' said Peter, 'you shall never wash my feet.' Jesus answered, 'Unless I wash you, you have no part with me.' 'Then, Lord,' Simon Peter replied, 'not just my feet but my hands and my head as well!' Jesus answered, 'A person who has had a bath needs only to wash his feet; his whole body is clean. And you are clean, though not every one of you'" (John 13:6-10).

Peter didn't need a bath. He had already been born again and cleansed of all his past sin. But even those who are clean before God pick up dirt on their feet, so to speak, by damaging their relationship with God as they commit new sins. Jesus was showing how even believers need ongoing forgiveness and cleansing.

The process is painful for Abigail. This illustrates how excruciating turning from sin can be. Even after we have made a decisive break with a sin at conversion, the process of the Lord cleaning up the mess from new sin can be painful. Her deformed feet represent the consequences of her sin and dealing with those consequences can often hurt.

For example, suppose a drunk finally repents and gives up drinking. He is restored to fellowship with God, but he has conditioned his body to crave alcohol, and each time that craving hits and he has to resist it, it will be painful.

Chapter 22 Meanings

Abigail's Smile

When Abigail appears with the Ruler and Father in the hall, her smile is identical to the Father's. This reflects the fact that our joy is the very happiness of God.

"I have told you this so that my joy may be in you and that your joy may be complete" (John 15:11).

Her smile is the brightest in the hall, illustrating that those who have been forgiven much, love much (Luke 7:47).

Flinging the Doors Open

The people who refuse to forgive Abigail open the doors of the hall, allowing the evil spirits entry. This shows how unforgiving people (or people in any other kind of unrepentant sin) invite satanic influence into the church. Sin gives a place to the devil both in the believer's life and in the church (Ephesians 4:27).

Watson vs. the Prince

When Watson confronts Hodia, a guardian remarks, "He has no idea," meaning Watson was unaware that he was facing off with the prince of darkness himself.

Watson's approach is a model for how Scripture teaches us to confront those in sin. He begins with the "dagger" of admonition, pointing out her fault (Matthew 18:15).

When that doesn't work, he steps up to rebuke. "This is how we know who the children of the Father are and who the children of the prince of darkness are—anyone who does not love her sister is a child of darkness. … You are behaving like Cain, who belonged to the evil one and murdered his brother. And why did he murder him? Because his own actions were evil and his brother's were righteous. Anyone who hates her sister is a murderer, and you know that no murderer has eternal life" (see 1 John 3:10-12).

Watson's Death

After Watson is crushed to death, guardians escort him to the Ruler. This reflects the account of the poor beggar, Lazarus, who was carried by angels to Abraham's side when he died (Luke 16:22).

Watson is full of joy, and he can hardly remember what anxiety, fear, worry, and boredom felt like. This is to describe the paradise Christ promised believers the day they die (Luke 23:43). The river of delights comes from Psalm 36:8.

Levi doesn't understand why the friends aren't grieving more for Watson. Charles explains that they don't grieve like the lowlanders because Watson's death is temporary, like sleep. And whoever loses his life for the Ruler will save it.

"Brothers, we do not want you to be ignorant about those who fall asleep, or to grieve like the rest of men, who have no hope. We believe that Jesus died and rose again and so we believe that God will bring with Jesus those who have fallen asleep in him" (1 Thessalonians 4:13-14).

"Whoever finds his life will lose it, and whoever loses his life for my sake will find it" (Matthew 10:39).

Charles quotes the Ruler. "I am the resurrection and the life. He who believes in me will live, even though he dies. And whoever lives and believes in me will never die" (see John 11:25-26).

Chapter 23 Meanings

Memories of the Ruler

Charles knows he should get up and meet with the Ruler, but his flesh wants to stay in bed—until he remembers some stories about the Ruler.

"During the days of his weakness, he offered up prayers and petitions with loud cries and tears to the one who could save him from death, and he was heard because of his reverent submission. Let us then approach the throne of the Father's favor with confidence, so we may receive mercy and find life from the Father to help us in our time of need" (see Hebrews 5:7, 4:16).

"Do not be anxious about anything, but in everything, by prayer and petition, present your requests to the Father, and his peace, which transcends understanding, will guard your heart and mind through your friendship with the Ruler" (see Philippians 4:6-7).

"As the deer pants for streams of water, so my soul pants for the Ruler. My body longs for him in a dry and weary land where there is no water. When can I go and meet with him? Why are you downcast, O my soul, why so disturbed within me? Put your hope in the Father, for I will yet trust him, my Savior and my God" (see Psalms 42:1-2,5-6).

Chapter 24 Meanings

The Map Room

The map room represents biblical prophecy. The Ruler gathers the friends in the map room to show them his plans.

Levi is shocked to discover the Ruler was the sovereign power behind everything, including the collapse of the hall. Sometimes people imagine God is not in control of negative events. But Scripture is clear that God is in sovereign control of all things.

"When times are good, be happy; but when times are bad, consider: God has made the one as well as the other" (Ecclesiastes 7:14).

"Is it not from the mouth of the Most High that both calamities and good things come?" (Lamentations 3:38)

The ruler explains to Charles that his hall was not wrecked but cleansed. The factions were necessary to show who has his approval.

"No doubt there have to be differences among you to show which of you have God's approval" (1 Corinthians 11:19).

Bad to Worse

The ruler tells of a time when the orchard will go from bad to worse. Appetites will become more and more perverse. This comes from 2 Timothy 3:13.

Long Delay

The Ruler warns the friends to be ready at any time, but also to be prepared for a long delay. This is the point of the parable of the virgins, where some are not ready for the Lord's return because he takes so long (see Matthew 25:1-13).

Co-Ruling

The Ruler tells the friends of a time when they will reign with him over a glorious kingdom. The idea of God's people reigning with him is perhaps the most central theme of the whole Bible (see 2 Timothy 2:12).

Dear Reader,

Thanks for reading! I pray you were edified by the story. If so, would you consider taking a quick moment to go to wherever you purchased this book and leave a review? A sentence or two is fine. It really helps others find the book.

I'd love to hear your impressions. Please send me a text at (720) 593-9985□ and let me know what you thought.

And if you'd like to be alerted for future releases, text your email address to that same number and I'll add you to my Reader's List.

The end

Claim your free short story!

Hannah's Prayer: Dawn from Desolation
How one desperate prayer rattled heaven and changed the world.

Part 1 of the Life of David Series from 1 & 2 Samuel.

Get a free download of Hannah's Prayer when you sign up for D. Richard Ferguson's Reader's Group at www.DRichardFerguson.com

Made in United States
Orlando, FL
21 November 2022